Noodle Pie

Noodle Pie

Ruth Starke

Kane Miller
A DIVISION OF EDC PUBLISHING

First American Edition 2010
Kane Miller, A Division of EDC Publishing

First published in 2008 by Omnibus Books, Scholastic Australia
Text copyright © Ruth Starke 2008

Jacket design: Kat Godard, DraDog, LLC.
Cover photo of Vietnamese youth on scooters: Denise Couturier

For information contact:
Kane Miller, A Division of EDC Publishing
P.O. Box 470663
Tulsa, OK 74147-0663
www.kanemiller.com
www.edcpub.com

Library of Congress Control Number: 2009931231

Manufactured by Regent Publishing Services, Hong Kong
Printed September 2010 in ShenZhen, Guangdong, China
1 2 3 4 5 6 7 8 9 10

ISBN: 978-1-935279-25-9

For my father

Acknowledgments

I began to think about this story during two visits to Vietnam in 2003 and 2004, but was able to begin writing it thanks to a Varuna Retreat Fellowship in 2005. In the following year, I was able to complete the manuscript when the May Gibbs Children's Literature Trust granted me a three-week Brisbane residency under its Fellowship program.

Thank you to many Australian and Vietnamese friends and colleagues for help, advice and encouragement during the writing of this novel. In Hanoi: Gail Parr, Library Manager, Australian Development Scholarships Project Center; Long Dinh, Australian Embassy; Pham Cong Tuoc (Duke), friend and guide; Duong Thi Thu, Win Hotel; Maria, John, Chi and Thanh, dining companions; and Phuong, a Viet Kieu who told me his refugee story as we cruised Ha Long Bay. In Australia: Pam Macintyre, first reader and best critic; Petra

Starke, fellow traveler and webpage designer; Judith Russell and Nan Halliday, state coordinators, May Gibbs Children's Literature Trust; Dyan Blacklock and Penny Matthews, publisher and editor. Thanks also to Graham Holliday, whose lively and informative Saigon-based street food blog Noodlepie.com inspired my title.

Chapter 1

According to Andy's father, they were going home. As the Vietnam Airlines jet began its descent he gazed out the window. "The last time I see that coastline," he said, "I was squashed inside a rusty fishing boat with sixty other people, heading out to sea. No room to stretch out or lie down, nothing to do for three days and nights. Waves very high. Water slosh in around our feet all time. Everyone seasick. Everyone praying we won't sink or be raided by pirates."

The first time Andy had heard that story, he'd imagined the kind of pirates he'd read about in books or seen on the screen: dashing dudes wearing frilly shirts and brandishing cutlasses.

"Three times we were raided," his father went on. "When we reach Thailand, we have only the clothes on our backs.

Officials in refugee camp search us again, looking for money and gold to steal, but we tell them, 'We have nothing left! Pirates take it all.'" His father laughed, as if he were telling an amusing story.

Perhaps it seemed funny to him now because it all happened so long ago, Andy thought. But it couldn't have been very funny at the time, especially when you were barely fifteen years old and on your own. His father never talked much about that time in his life, and he'd never been back to the country of his birth before.

"What would happen if you went back to Vietnam, Dad?" Andy had asked him once, years ago.

"They would lock me up. Maybe shoot me."

"Why?"

"Because my family anti-communist and because I escape."

Yet here they were, going back. Well, Andy wasn't. He'd been born in Australia. For him the trip wasn't a going back, it was a going *to*.

He looked out the window at the green coastline and the vastness of the ocean, and tried to imagine himself doing what his father had done. He'd be scared, he knew that. He wasn't even sure he'd be brave enough to leave home in the first place. But if his father had stayed in Vietnam, he, Andrew Nguyen, aged eleven years and seven months, wouldn't be sitting here now, flying into Hanoi with an Australian passport in his pocket. His father had an Australian passport too. That was probably the reason it was now safe for him to go back.

When the "Fasten Seatbelts" sign came on, Andy obediently clicked his seatbelt into place. To many of the Vietnamese on board, however, the sign seemed to convey another message entirely, one that said, "Beat the rush and get ready now." They jumped to their feet and opened overhead compartments. They pulled down bags and parcels, and put on hats and jackets. They jostled in the aisles, their faces tense and eager, as if they were in a race and they were only waiting for the plane to touch down before they sprinted for the door.

Andy looked at them disapprovingly. Didn't they realize this was the most dangerous time of the entire flight? Hadn't they read the safety and emergency evacuation guides in their seat pockets?

"They should stay in their seats until we come to a complete stop," he said to his father. "We could hit an air pocket, the wheels might not come down, the pilot might miss the runway, a bird could fly into the windshield —"

"They excited to be coming home," his father said. "And for some, maybe first time in airplane."

"It's my first flight, too," Andy said. "But I still know the safety rules."

"Smart boy. Not everybody have your education," his father said.

Andy didn't think it had anything to do with education. He'd noted how the Vietnamese had pushed their way onto the plane, elbowing past other passengers, taking all the space in the overhead compartments and under the seats. Now they seemed determined to be the first ones off. Vietnamese, he concluded, were just selfish and impatient. If he got around to writing a travel diary, that would be his first entry.

His father had said it was a good idea to write everything down in a travel diary. "Then you don't forget all the different happenings and can tell your mother and your friends everything when you get home."

If he wanted to tell his mother and friends what he was doing – and Andy wasn't sure that he could be bothered – there was always email.

Vietnam had heaps of cheap internet cafes, according to his teacher, Mrs. Gowdie, who had been there last year on a Discovery Tour. He wasn't interested in keeping a daily diary. But observations – he was good at those. Last term, for Science, Mrs. Gowdie had made everyone keep an Observations notebook ("Science is about observing and drawing conclusions from those observations"), and he'd gotten the highest mark for his. Nobody else in the class had recorded so many different observations on hopping mice, Mrs. Gowdie said.

The captain's voice on the intercom ordered everybody to sit down and buckle up. Flight attendants scuttled down the aisles, and eventually everyone was persuaded to resume their seats. There was a buzz of excitement and babies started to howl as the patchwork land loomed closer and closer.

Andy's father seemed nervous. He licked his lips as he peered out the window, and he twisted and turned the ring on his finger. It was new, a thick gold ring, studded with diamonds. Noticing it for the first time, Andy stared. The gold watch on his father's wrist was new, too. When had he acquired such luxuries? He certainly hadn't had them when they left home. Perhaps he'd bought them at the Duty Free shop, where expensive things were supposed to be really cheap. Normally his father would never dream of spending money on jewelry, especially for himself. For as long as Andy could remember, he had worn a battered old Timex.

"Pretty flashy." Andy said, pointing. "When did you get them?"

"Where are your shoes?" his father asked, ignoring the question.

"Under the seat in front. I can't get them without unbuckling my seatbelt, and I don't think I should do that. This is the most dangerous time – "

"Find them and put them on."

Andy unbuckled his seatbelt and scrabbled around on the floor. He hoped the flight attendants couldn't see him. They'd think he was another of those ignorant Vietnamese passengers. He located his sneakers and struggled to put them on. It was difficult in the confined space. He couldn't bend down properly and his feet seemed to have grown a size since he'd left home. If the plane hit an air pocket now, he'd bounce up sharply and hit his head on the "Fasten Seatbelts" sign.

He managed to tie his laces and straightened up, his face flushed. His father glanced at him critically, and frowned when he noticed the stains on the front of his T-shirt.

"It's from when I opened that can of Coke," Andy explained. "It must be the air pressure or something. The same thing happened with the orange juice. And those little tubs of milk. And the mineral water, but you can't see that." He rubbed ineffectually at his T-shirt. That was another observation: airline liquids sealed with foil exploded when opened at altitude. Airlines should use screw tops. If he saw the pilot, he'd mention it to him.

"You can put jacket on after we land." His father had hardly moved from his seat during the long flight, and there wasn't a single wrinkle in his dark suit pants, or his white business shirt, or his tie. All new, all bought for the trip home. Andy wondered why he had chosen such uncomfortable clothes to travel in. At home on weekends, when he wasn't working, he wore jeans or sweatpants, and sitting for hours in a plane seat watching a little screen was pretty much like sitting in a chair in your family room watching television. A more uncomfortable chair, of course.

A flight attendant headed down the aisle towards them.

Andy reached quickly for his seatbelt, but he was sitting on one half of it and was forced to do a little jig in his seat. Caught out! Now he'd be reprimanded in front of the entire Economy section. Well, rows 40 to 55, anyway. How embarrassing.

The flight attendant didn't seem to notice that he wasn't buckled in. She handed his father his suit jacket, which he'd given to her to hang up when they'd boarded the flight. "Here you are, Mr. Nguyen," she said in Vietnamese. She smiled at Andy and asked his name.

Before he could reply, his father told her. "Nguyen Cuong Anh."

We haven't even landed in the country, but already he's calling me by my Vietnamese name. Fastening his seatbelt, Andy said, "My name's Andrew Nguyen." And then he added, in Vietnamese, "I'm Australian." He wasn't sure why he wanted to tell her that. Perhaps it was just to let her know that he could speak Vietnamese.

"Is this your first visit to Vietnam?" she asked.

Andy nodded. Two years ago his mother had taken his younger sister Mai with her to visit her family in Saigon, and now it was his turn. He said, "We're visiting my father's family in Hanoi." *His* family, too, of course, although he'd never met any of them.

"You'll have a lot to talk about," the flight attendant said. "I bet there'll be a crowd to welcome you at the airport."

"Big crowd," said his father. "First time home for us both."

The flight attendant said something to him in Vietnamese that Andy didn't understand, but he nodded intelligently as if he did.

As she walked back down the aisle, he was suddenly nervous. The truth was, his Vietnamese wasn't that good. At home he talked to his parents in a mixture of both languages – what he called "Vietlish" – although it was more English than Vietnamese. He knew his grandparents didn't speak English. Would he be able to understand them? Would they understand him? He'd forget what little he did know and be tongue-tied. Or he'd say something really stupid, which was easy to do in Vietnamese, because one word could mean several different things, depending on how you pronounced it. For example, you might *think* you were asking someone to pass the salt, but what you were actually saying was "Pass me the nose," or "Pass me ten" or "Pass me the smell." The same word meant all four things. It was a lazy language, Andy thought, and unnecessarily complicated.

"Got your passport?" his father asked.

Yes, of course I've got my passport. You've asked me at least a dozen times since we left home. He pulled it out of his pocket. His father had wanted to carry it in his travel wallet along with their tickets and other documents, but Andy had stubbornly refused to surrender it. If he was old enough to have his own passport, he was old enough to be responsible for it.

He pulled out the duplicated Customs form he'd signed earlier and started to read the small print on the back. No, he wasn't bringing any guns, explosives, knives or pornographic material into the country – unlike the blonde girl two rows to his left who was stuffing a copy of *Cosmo* into her shoulder bag. He could see cleavage on the cover and some headlines. "Your Best Legs." "The Daily Kiss." Customs would be on to that like a shot. She really ought to leave the magazine on the plane.

He was just about to lean over and suggest this to her when something else on the form caught his eye. Also prohibited were "children's toys having negative effects on personality development." He showed it to his father. "What does this mean?"

His father read it and shrugged. "Who knows? War games, violent computer games, perhaps. Vietnam has communist government, remember. There's a lot of censorship."

Andy thought of the Game Boy in their hand luggage. They'd bought it in the Duty Free shop for his cousin, Hien. He reminded his father, who shook his head and said, "I don't think Customs would confiscate that."

Andy certainly hoped not. First of all, it had cost heaps, and second, how could a Game Boy possibly have a negative effect on development?

Computer games were excellent for improving hand and eye coordination. Even Mrs. Fossey at school, who considered most modern technology more trouble than it was worth, admitted that.

He tried to think of toys that the Vietnamese government might not approve of. All he could come up with was Barbie. She was pretty decadent, with all her clothes and sports cars and houses with swimming pools. A lot of Vietnamese didn't even have a bicycle or running water, his father had told him. No, communists wouldn't look kindly on Barbie.

"Did Mai take her Barbie to Saigon?" he asked. "I reckon we would have heard the scream in Australia if Customs had tried to take it from her."

His father wasn't paying attention. He peered out the window intently as, with a slight bump and jolt, the plane landed. Many of the passengers applauded, as if complimenting the pilot on a job well done. As if he could hear them way up in the cockpit! All around him Andy heard the *snap, snap, snap* of seatbelts.

"We're home," his father said.

Chapter 2

Both of them were surprised at how clean and modern Noi Bai airport was. It wasn't like a Third World airport at all, Andy thought. Not that he'd seen any others, but he'd imagined sheds and open tarmacs and beggars, maybe even a cow or two. No, that was India.

His father seemed even more nervous than he had been on the plane. As they waited in line at Immigration, he glanced around him and constantly wiped his hands on his trousers – those immaculate trousers he'd kept so clean and uncreased all the way from Australia. Perhaps he was worried in case they had the wrong visas. Or   the thought jumped into Andy's head and he wondered why it had never occurred to him before – perhaps there was a sort of immigration "black list" that contained the name of every refugee who had fled from

Vietnam since 1975, when the war ended. Was that why he had bought a diamond ring and a flashy watch and dressed in a new suit? To convince the authorities that he was now a powerful businessman? He wasn't, of course. Far from it. But he looked very nice.

Their turn came. They stepped up to the booth and presented their passports to a granite-faced official in a green uniform shirt. Andy felt his own palms begin to sweat as the man stared at their photos, and then at them, and then at the photos again. Andy was about to explain that the reason he looked like a startled rabbit in his photo was because he was trying not to sneeze. He had felt it coming on just as the photographer had squeezed the shutter, and had held his breath in an effort to stop it.

He decided not to say anything. The man might not speak English, and he certainly didn't have the Vietnamese words for all that.

After what seemed a long time, the official stamped their passports, shoved them across the desk and rather grumpily waved them through.

"He wasn't very friendly, was he?" Andy said.

"I didn't expect him to be," his father said.

"The government ought to encourage people like him to smile and say in a friendly voice, 'Welcome to Vietnam. Have a nice stay,'" Andy said. First impressions were very important, especially in the tourism industry.

He ran ahead to grab a cart, but it took a long time

for their baggage to appear on the carousel. It stopped and started, got jammed, and then jerked and hiccupped into temporary life before stopping again a few minutes later. His father kept glancing anxiously behind them, as luckier passengers who had already claimed their luggage went through Customs. Andy spotted the *Cosmo* girl and watched with interest to see how she'd react when she was arrested. She wasn't, and passed through with minimum delay.

That was a good sign, Andy decided. Then he noticed that Customs seemed more interested in examining the baggage of returning Vietnamese. Admittedly, most of them had enough stuff to fill a semi-trailer, but it seemed a bad sign. His father had noticed, too.

"Are you worried about the Game Boy?" Andy asked.

"I'm not worried about the Game Boy."

"What *are* you worried about then?" Andy asked in a low voice. Had his father packed something he didn't know about?

His father gave a little laugh. "The Customs and Immigration officers in their green uniforms remind me of soldiers, that's all. I keep expecting to get arrested."

"You've got an Australian passport," Andy reminded him.

"Yes. I am being silly."

Andy thought of another reason it was important for airport officials to smile and look welcoming: so returning refugees like his father didn't feel nervous or threatened.

Eventually their baggage arrived on the carousel and they loaded everything onto a cart together with their hand luggage, and pushed it towards Customs. An officer took their passports and looked at their declaration forms. He ran an eye over their baggage. There was so much of it that Andy expected him to ask how many years they were planning to stay.

He said something in Vietnamese and Andy recognized the words "gifts for family." His heart gave a little jump. They had heaps of gifts in their bags, not to mention that enormous electric rice cooker, boxed and wrapped in plastic and twine. But electric rice cookers would hardly be on a list of prohibited imports. It was that Game Boy they had to worry about. Should they declare it now and hope for a lighter sentence? What *was* the fine for importing negative children's toys, anyway? Andy knew his face had turned pink, and he was sure beads of sweat had broken out on his forehead. What a pathetic drug smuggler he'd make. Not that he'd ever, ever do anything like that, of course.

His father turned to him and said, "Anh, this man wants me to go with him. I won't be long. You stay here."

"No way. I'll come too," Andy said. The Game Boy was all his idea. His father had wanted to buy a watch for Hien. If anyone was going to be arrested, it ought to be him, Andy.

His father started to protest, but the Customs man was looking impatient, so he sighed and said, "All right, but don't say anything."

They followed the officer into a small room that contained only a desk and two chairs. It was probably the room where they searched suspects for drugs, Andy thought. The Customs officer ignored the chairs and began talking in rapid Vietnamese. Andy had difficulty following much of it, but he understood the words "coffee money." He waited for his father to tell the man they didn't want coffee, thanks very much, they just wanted to get out of the airport.

There was an exchange of words, and then his father, with a tense expression on his face, reached for his wallet. He took out an American ten-dollar bill and offered it to the officer. It seemed a lot for coffee, but apparently it wasn't enough. The man shook his head. He said something, and again Andy caught the word "family." Was he talking about his own family, or theirs?

His father added another ten-dollar bill, and this time the officer took it. He folded the money and put it in his pocket. They all trooped back to the Customs station. The officer ripped off the top copy of their declaration forms, handed them the yellow duplicates, and waved his hand.

"That's it?" Andy murmured to his father. "We can go?"

"We can go," his father said, seizing the luggage cart and heading for the exit.

"What was that all about? Why did he want money to buy coffee?"

"Nothing to do with coffee. Just a little phrase they use."

"But you gave him twenty dollars."

"So he not search our bags."

"Ha! You *were* worried about the Game Boy!"

His father shook his head. "No, to save time. He knows

we have family waiting outside. He say if I don't pay, he go through all our bags very slowly and keep us there for an hour or two."

"Is he allowed to do that?"

His father shrugged. "People warned me it would happen. Many people here trying to make extra money. Especially from tourists and Viet Kieu."

"What's Viet Kieu?"

"I am Viet Kieu," his father said. "It's the name for overseas Vietnamese, people who were born here but left to live in other countries."

"So I'm not a Viet Kieu?"

"You son of Viet Kieu. Don't know the word for that."

"I do," Andy said. "It's Australian. That's what I am."

"Okay. But to my family, you are Vietnamese. Others here will think you are Viet Kieu."

Andy opened his mouth to ask him why, but they'd reached the Arrivals hall and his father was no longer listening to him. Grinning from ear to ear, he was waving to a large group of people who were jumping up and down, clutching huge bunches of red roses, and waving back at him.

At both of them. *This is your family, Andy.*

So many of them. How would he ever remember all their names?

His father abandoned the cart and rushed around the barrier towards them. Andy hung back, not only because he felt a bit shy but because he knew that his father should be greeted first. On the plane he'd explained to his son about what he called "circles of welcome." Now Andy could almost tell who was who by where people were standing and in what order they came forward to greet his father. The most senior member – his grandmother – would be at the very front, and then would come Auntie Mo, his father's elder sister, and Uncle Hop, her husband, and then other uncles and aunts ranked in order of importance. They would be followed by cousins, by age and gender, and after them would come great-aunts and great-uncles and second and third cousins and goodness knows who else.

It made Andy feel funny inside to say – even to himself – "my grandmother," "my aunt," "my cousins," and to see them all there in front of him. He looked to the very back of the group to see who was considered the least important family member. She wasn't tall, so he didn't see her until somebody moved. She had short hair and bangs down to her eyebrows. There was a sullen expression on her small, triangular face, or maybe she was just bored. It couldn't have been much fun hanging around the airport all this time.

The girl saw him looking at her and, even at a distance, Andy caught the quick flash of defiance in her dark eyes. She wrinkled her nose at him, stuck out her tongue, and pulled a cheeky face. Taken by surprise, Andy didn't know whether to laugh or feel offended. There was something about the girl that reminded him of Mai. Then the people in front moved again and she disappeared.

His father's arms were full of roses and he looked as if
he might be about to cry. Andy had never seen him look so
emotional, not even when his mother and Mai returned from
Saigon. Not even when Vietnam defeated Singapore in the
Sea Games Soccer Cup.

Somebody called out his name. It was his Auntie Mo. Her
black, bird eyes behind her glasses rapidly looked him over,
like an experienced shopper contemplating a purchase. She
touched him on the forearm – a welcoming gesture – and
thrust a bunch of roses at him. Andy managed a muttered
"Thank you" in Vietnamese. She beamed, as if he had just said
something terribly complicated and clever. The smile softened
her face.

Andy held the roses awkwardly. He felt like a dork, and he
was glad that Dizzy and Hendo back home couldn't see him.
Nobody had ever given him flowers before.

Auntie Mo pushed him towards his grandmother. The old
woman seized him in a fierce embrace that crushed the roses
against his new jacket. Andy didn't understand a word she was
saying, but he assumed it was words of welcome. He recited
the formal greeting his father had drummed into his head.

His grandmother gave him a wide smile and let loose a
stream of Vietnamese. Andy was shocked to see that her teeth
were stained black.

"She say you very big and tall, Anh," Auntie Mo said.

He supposed he was, compared to his grandmother. But
then, everybody in Australia over the age of about nine would

be too. Slender and wiry, she barely came up to his shoulder. Her still-dark hair was parted in the middle and drawn back smoothly into a knot on her neck. She was certainly strong; she held Andy's hand in a grip of iron, and hardly let anyone else near him.

His grandfather was not at the airport, but Andy had expected that. He hadn't been well for a long time and would greet them at home. There were lots of medicines in their luggage for him. And toothpaste, Andy suddenly remembered, although dental hygiene might have come too late for his grandmother.

They went outside. It was late in the afternoon and the sky was heavy and grey. There was a grittiness, like fine grade sandpaper, in the air. His father sniffed and smiled, but Andy couldn't smell anything special, just gas and diesel fumes. Immediately they were surrounded by hustling taxi drivers, but Auntie Mo yelled at them and waved them away. "We have minibus," she explained.

Everybody piled into it. Andy was seated up front, just behind the driver, so he wouldn't miss anything. He wondered how they were all going to fit, but somehow they did. The cheeky girl was somewhere at the back, sitting on the suitcases. Nobody had even introduced her.

They drove out of the airport and turned onto a busy highway. Traffic whizzed past in both directions, but their driver was unfazed. He charged into the middle of the stream, blasted his horn, and gunned the engine. Trucks bore down on them, and scooters and motorbikes, most overloaded with passengers, weaved in and out of their slipstream. The driver lit a cigarette and blasted his horn every few seconds. Andy nearly jumped out of his skin at the sound. It seemed to belong to a fifty-ton truck rather than a minibus, but it didn't impress the taxi in front, which refused to move over or go faster. Their driver leaned on the horn again, and flashed his lights. Andy wasn't sure what the hurry was. They were already doing more than the speed limit. Any minute they'd get pulled over by a traffic cop.

Were there any traffic cops? Nobody on the highway was driving as if there were, and none of his relatives seemed worried about imminent death. They shouted at each other over the noise of the engine and the roar of the traffic, and passed around bottles of water.

Soon they were speeding past green fields where women in conical straw hats tended buffalo and waded ankle-deep in water, planting or cutting rice.

A jet swooped low over the paddy fields, coming in to land. Jet power and manpower, Andy thought. He ought to take a photo, because this was what Mrs. Gowdie called "irony." It would make an excellent shot. But his new digital camera was tucked away in his backpack. His father had said you could get arrested for taking photos in or around the airport.

Along the edges of the highway, risking death at every turn of the wheels, children pedaled home from school on old bicycles that at home would be thrown out for the trash collectors. They carried their books in plastic baskets hooked over the handlebars – even the boys.

Ragged farmers herded lines of plodding oxen as girls wearing *ao dai* whizzed by on scooters, their arms covered by elbow-length gloves and everything below the eyes hidden behind scarves or masks. People carried the most amazing loads on their bikes, like bamboo cages crammed with ducks, or huge pieces of machinery. A man on a motorcycle zipped past, a live pig trussed and strapped to the pillion. At least, Andy assumed it was alive. He wished again he could take a photo.

"Look at that, Anh," his father said, pointing to two cyclists riding side by side, hauling a large sofa between them.

I wish he'd call me Andy, like he does at home.

The rice paddies gave way to ramshackle villages, but there were also some big houses that looked nothing at all like Australian houses. They were tall and narrow, like matchboxes standing on end, and made of concrete painted in pastel colors of orange, pink and blue. They stood three stories high, with open terraces under tiled pagoda-like roofs where lines of washing flapped. Andy thought of their three-bedroom bungalow in Adelaide, with the rotary clothesline in the backyard.

The minibus turned off the highway onto a dusty, potholed track lined with shacks. The driver must have lost his way, Andy thought, this couldn't be the way into the city.

But yes, it was. A new road was under construction. It was obviously going to take some time because most of it was being done by hand. Laborers smashed boulders with picks and lugged stones in flat bamboo baskets. Andy was shocked to see that some of the workers were women.

They drove under a concrete bridge where a market was being held on a piece of dusty wasteland. Well, a sort of market. There weren't any stalls. Goods for sale – mostly junky-looking bits of clothing and shoes – were arranged in heaps on plastic sheets on the ground. People drifted around, looking and buying. Another piece of striped plastic, held up by four bamboo poles, served as a cafe. Customers sat around on little toy-sized plastic stools, eating and drinking.

"Is this Hanoi?" Andy asked.

Everyone in the minibus laughed uproariously. "Ha-ha! He thinks this is Hanoi!"

Andy felt his cheeks grow hot. *Well, how do I know? This is the Third World, isn't it? I bet the girl at the back's killing herself.*

"First we cross Red River," said Uncle Hop. "Then we in Hanoi, Old Quarter."

They drove on, then crossed a big bridge over a river that was muddy, not red. Suddenly they were driving along crowded tree-lined streets where the houses had shutters and little balconies, and every second building was a shop. There were cafes and roadside markets and food stalls. Women in conical straw hats carried heavy shoulder baskets filled with bananas and oranges and vegetables. Hundreds of parked motorbikes lined both sides of the narrow sidewalks, and goods tumbled out of open shop fronts. Wherever there was a tiny bit of space it was occupied by either a skinny man tinkering with a motorbike or a skinny woman squatting to cook something over a charcoal fire or a few sticks of burning wood – right there on the roadside, amid all the dust and refuse and traffic fumes. Andy was shocked. Where were the health inspectors?

The traffic here was at least twenty times worse, and so were the noise and danger levels. Everybody beeped their horns constantly and nobody wore a crash helmet. Street signs and traffic lights seemed nonexistent. Cars, trucks, vans, cyclos, scooters and motorbikes, up to ten abreast and often laden with passengers or household goods, zigzagged and zoomed around blind corners, narrowly missing each other and any pedestrians suicidal enough to try crossing the road. It was a bit like turning off a country lane and suddenly finding yourself in the middle of a mad Grand Prix.

"Rush hour?" he heard his father ask.

"It is always like this," Uncle Hop said.

Andy wondered if vehicles here had brakes and signals. The horn was used for everything: passing, turning left, turning right, warning other drivers, frightening pedestrians. It seemed to be illegal to drive in Hanoi without beeping your horn every fifteen seconds.

They drove through the Old Quarter and around a lake called Hoan Kiem, with a little temple in the middle, and trees and flowers and cafes. Behind him, Auntie Mo tapped Andy on the shoulder and said she came here for her early morning exercise classes. "You can come with me, Anh," she said.

You must be joking.

The minibus sped carelessly across a busy intersection, turned into a tree-lined street, and jerked to a stop outside a narrow three-story building with a curved red tile roof, one in a row of similar shophouses.

"Welcome home, Anh," said his grandmother, in English. Andy looked at her in surprise. She giggled shyly.

"Everyone been learning English," said Auntie Mo.

Well, thank goodness for that, Andy thought.

Chapter 3

Everybody piled out of the minibus and helped to unload the luggage. Andy's father took out his wallet. Grandma squawked and waved it away. The driver had already been paid. What did he think? That she would come to the airport to greet her only son and let him pay for the taxi home? His father gave the driver some money anyway. The driver looked very happy, and sped off.

"Too much," scolded Grandma.

"Viet Kieu!" exclaimed Auntie Mo, and everybody laughed, including Andy's father.

Andy knew it wasn't the same as at the airport. This money was a tip, even though he'd never seen his father tip back home. Usually he counted every cent. He looked for his backpack, but Cheeky Girl had already grabbed it. An older cousin snatched it away and snapped at her, as if she had no right to handle anything so important.

Andy was about to say that he'd carry his own backpack, thanks all the same, when he suddenly realized where they were.

This was the family restaurant. Phuong Nguyen.

He stared. It wasn't really a restaurant at all. It was a narrow-fronted shop which opened right out onto the street. The sign above the entrance said *Cac Mon An* and *Com Binh Dan*, which meant something like "All kinds of food" and "Plain home cooking." There was a small counter and a sort of metal cart stacked high with dishes and plastic bowls and buckets, and some empty Coke crates for additional storage. Behind all this clutter, in a room about the size of Andy's bedroom, were a couple of folding tables and chairs. Mounted on the walls were some framed prints, two electric fans and a color television set. The tiled floor looked like it needed a good scrub.

His father had a nerve, calling this a restaurant. It was hardly even a cafe.

Andy had boasted about it at school. "Oh yeah, my grandma has this really famous restaurant in Hanoi. Phuong Nguyen, named after her. Everybody eats there." He'd imagined something like the elegant restaurant in the Botanic Gardens where his father worked, or the popular Saigon Palace near the market, where they'd celebrated his mother's last birthday.

Dizzy and Hendo would laugh themselves sick if they could see this place.

He stared at his father accusingly. He ought to be looking suitably embarrassed at the whoppers he'd been telling over the years. Instead, his father was gazing around him in cheerful amazement. "Bicycles and pajamas," he said. "Where have they gone?"

"What?" Andy said.

"All changed, all different. Streets used to be shady and quiet. People walked or rode bicycles, very few cars about. Now streets full of noise and Hondas and crazy traffic."

"Hanoi same-same, but different," said Uncle Hop. "Only countryside never change."

"Our house is the best in the street, thanks to you, Brother," said Auntie Mo.

What did that mean? Andy wondered. Had his father paid for the house, or helped pay for it? And if so, did his mother know, and where had the money come from? They weren't rich.

He tugged his father's sleeve. "This isn't really a restaurant, is it?" he asked in a low voice.

His father turned his attention to the Phuong Nguyen. "Sure it is," he said heartily – a little too heartily, thought Andy, who hadn't missed the fleeting look of surprise in his eyes.

"It's not like restaurants at home."

His father smiled. "Same-same but different. Nothing here exactly like things at home."

"But it's not a bit like you said it was," Andy insisted. "It's not a restaurant, it's a … a …" He didn't know what it was.

"Sshh," his father said.

A boy a little younger than Andy came out of the small kitchen at the back. It was his cousin Hien. He wore sweatpants and a T-shirt, which seemed to displease Auntie Mo. She poked him in the chest and let him have an earful. Andy could guess what she was saying: exactly what his own mother would say. "Why are you wearing those old clothes? I told you to get dressed for the visitors. Blah, blah, blah..."

Barely listening to her, Hien said, "Yeah, yeah, Ma."

Andy wouldn't have changed his clothes either. *He looks a bit like me except I'm taller and our hair is different.*

Auntie Mo gave her son a fierce prod between the shoulders.

"Hello, welcome, Anh," Hien muttered.

"Hi. Call me Andy."

"What's my name in English?"

Surprised, Andy thought for a moment. There was no real equivalent. What started with H? "Henry," he suggested. "Hector? Homer?"

"They cool names, Andy?"

"Nah." Andy thought again. "What about Harry? There's Harry Potter. Prince Harry. And Harrison Ford. You know, Indiana Jones."

His cousin's face lit up. "Indy! Yeah, call me Indy."

They seemed to have jumped from Harry to Indy, but who cared? Andy was just grateful that his cousin's English was better than his own Vietnamese. He looked around for Cheeky Girl to ask what her name was, but she had disappeared.

Home and restaurant seemed to be one. They piled the bags inside the entrance and went through a door on the left and down a hallway and into a sort of sitting room. Everyone slipped off their shoes. Andy bent down and awkwardly untied his sneakers. If he had to do this every time he entered a room, he was going to get a pair of flip-flops.

There was a hole in his left sock. He stared at it. How had that got there? He twisted his sock so that the hole was under his big toe instead of on top of it.

"Don't forget to bow," his father reminded him.

"I *know*," Andy said.

Inside, his grandfather was waiting to greet them. Andy hardly recognized him. Like his grandmother, he looked years older than in the framed photograph on the mantelpiece at home. The photographer had obviously smoothed out all their lines and wrinkles. Which was all right, Andy supposed, as he bowed deeply from the waist, but a bit of a shock for your relatives when they saw you in the flesh. Especially when they had no idea your teeth were black! And his grandfather had been sick. He looked frail, as if a puff of wind could blow him away. When he embraced Andy and took his hand, his body trembled and his skin felt like dead leaves.

The relatives crowded onto two long benches facing one another, and he and his father sat down, on either side of his grandparents, on a carved wooden platform. Andy felt as though he were on stage. He tucked his left foot under him.

"It turns into a bed at night," his father whispered.

Andy hoped he wouldn't be sleeping on it.

For what seemed the next hour everyone was brought forward and formally introduced, starting with those nearest to them on the benches and working backwards. There were over twenty people in the room, and it was hard for Andy to get all the relationships straight. His father would say, "Anh, this is Thi Nhai, the wife of Dong, the second son of my middle cousin Thuy," and Andy would think, *What does that make us? Second cousins?* He had no idea.

All his father's comments were passed along the platform and down the benches, like the game of Chinese Whispers. "My wife sends you best wishes and affection" probably came out the other end as "My wife sends you dead fishes and infection." If his father spoke at length, the translation got shorter and shorter as it radiated outwards. No wonder people at the back sometimes looked puzzled.

Cheeky Girl was the last to be introduced. Her name was Minh, and she was the daughter of his father's younger sister, Auntie Trieu.

"Is that why she's last?" Andy whispered to his father, as she was hustled aside and sent to the back of the room again. "Because she's a girl of the youngest girl?" He was getting a handle on this ranking business.

"Yes. Also because her mother is divorced."

"So what?" Andy asked.

"Divorce is shameful to family. Sshh."

"Why?" Dizzy's mother was divorced. Lots of kids in his class had parents who were divorced. Nobody seemed to find it shameful, or even embarrassing.

"Sshh," his father said again.

How was it Minh's fault that her parents were divorced? Andy hadn't particularly liked the cheeky girl, but it seemed unjust, however you looked at it. "What if she was a boy? Would she still be last?" he asked.

His father ignored him.

"What is Anh saying?" Grandma asked.

"He is curious about his relatives," his father said.

His grandmother beamed at him. Andy changed his mind about the toothpaste. He'd see that *all* of it went to his grandmother.

Was that it now? Had they met everyone? He yawned, and shifted uncomfortably on the wooden platform.

Aaargh! Who were all *these* people, pushing into the room?

"I heard that Tuoc is back home again," an old woman said. "I would like to see him."

"And staying in the family home, too," said another.

There were general nods and murmurs of approval.

"Friends and neighbors," his father explained. "People who knew me when I was growing up here. Won't take long."

Yes, it will, Andy thought resentfully. He was in a strange country where he barely spoke the language. He had traveled over 5,000 miles, hadn't slept for about twenty hours or washed since early this morning – not that he cared about that, but he was hot and sweaty – and he was sitting on a wooden platform in his socks, in front of dozens of strangers who were all staring at him. Staring at the hole in his left sock. He tucked his foot under him again.

They filed up – in order of rank, Andy supposed. They brought presents of cakes and sweets. They smiled at Andy and said, "Tuoc, is this your son? What a handsome boy!" They looked at his father and exclaimed, "How grand and prosperous you look, Tuoc. How well you've done in Australia."

Andy's grandparents glowed with pride.

Now Andy understood why his father had worn a dark suit, and a shirt and a tie. The gold watch and the diamond ring were making a big impression, too, of course. He wondered again where the jewelry had come from, and what all these people would say if they could see his father washing their ancient Toyota in his old sweatpants. Or sitting at the kitchen table with a pile of bills in front of him, and grumbling that they'd be broke in three months unless they *Cut Back*. "On what?" his mother always said. "On food? On rent? On gas and electricity?"

But somehow the money had been found for their air fares to Vietnam, and here they were, like Santa Claus with a bag full of presents to distribute.

Andy wasn't convinced that some of the stuff his parents had packed as gifts would be warmly received. Toothpaste, for instance. How thrilling could it be to get a tube of Colgate mint gel, even if your teeth did resemble black pegs? Very, as it turned out, and ditto for deodorant, shampoo and conditioner, bottles of headache pills and vitamins. Anything that bore a well-known brand name or was made in America or Australia got the thumbs up.

Andy watched with growing disapproval as the relatives began to divide the loot amongst themselves. His aunts and cousins fell upon the face creams and moisturizers, and fought over the perfume and cosmetics. His uncles snatched at the cartons of cigarettes. Auntie Mo bagged the Estée Lauder pack against strong opposition from Auntie Thuy, who had to settle for Nivea. A length of navy wool jersey almost brought the two of them to blows, until Auntie Thuy finally let it go. "Okay, you have. You need. Dark color hides fat rolls."

The status thing was obviously at work again. Andy was surprised at the snatching and grabbing, and the sharp words when somebody scored an item somebody else felt entitled to. They reminded him of a flock of seagulls flapping over the remains of a picnic. "They're a bit rude, aren't they?" he whispered to his father.

His father shrugged. "It's custom."

"They should just take what they've been given and say thank you."

"Sshh."

Despite the squabbles, everybody got something in the end. Even the neighbors left with a toothbrush each or a bar of scented soap.

Andy's grandfather cradled his cigarettes and bottle of whisky, while his grandmother seemed highly satisfied with her presents of a wool jacket for winter and the electric rice cooker. This was immediately taken into the kitchen and placed where everyone passing on the street could see it and be impressed. "Wow, would you take a look at that, the Nguyens have an electric rice cooker! Viet Kieu money, you know."

Indy was bowled over by his Game Boy, and the envy of all the cousins. They crowded around as Andy showed him how to play, but Indy didn't seem to need any instruction. He caught on fast.

Andy could see Minh hovering in the background. As the lowliest of the cousins, she was in line to get something relatively insignificant – a bar of chocolate maybe, or a pen. Which she seemed to expect, because her eyes were fixed on an enormous box of colored pens. It was a real artist's collection, a rainbow assortment of gel and felt-tip pens of every possible color gradation and type including neon, metallic, glitter and fluorescent.

There were enough pens to give one to every kid in the family, and probably every kid in the street. That was the idea. That was why his mother had bought the box.

He reached for the box of pens and beckoned Minh to come forward. She did so, shyly. He held it out to her. She reached in and took one pen – a purple one.

Andy shook his head, and held out the entire box. "All for you."

34

There was a collective intake of breath from the relatives. Auntie Mo clicked her tongue in disapproval. Andy's father raised his eyebrows. The other cousins looked mutinous.

Minh looked startled, then overjoyed, then fearful. She glanced around, as if expecting the box of pens to be whipped away at any moment. Andy, realizing that there was every chance of this happening, turned to his father and said, "Tell her that the pens are for her because I heard she draws very well."

"Does she? I never heard that," his father murmured.

Neither had Andy. But then, he had never heard anything about Minh. "It doesn't matter," he said. "I just want her to have the pens."

"Are you sure?"

Andy nodded. "Say that I'd like her to do a drawing for me to take home to Mum."

His father translated his words and there was a further buzz among the relatives.

Minh's eyes sparkled, and she reached out for the box of pens. As she turned to go, Auntie Mo snapped something at her. Minh colored, lowered her eyes, and recited a formal thank you to Andy.

Andy was annoyed at his aunt. Nobody else, including Auntie Mo herself, had thanked them, not even in the most casual way, so why was she making Minh do it? At home, he was rapped over the knuckles if he didn't say thank you when someone passed him the bread, let alone gave him a present, but nobody here seemed very concerned about expressing their gratitude.

It must be one of those cultural differences Mrs. Gowdie went on about at school.

Minh finished her recitation and, hugging the box of pens to her chest, resumed her place at the back.

There was a strained silence in the room, broken only by the *tap-tap-tap* of Indy's Game Boy.

Good one, Andy thought. What a great start. Twenty of his relatives in the room, and eighteen of them probably wanted to strangle him.

Chapter 4

"Did I do wrong, Dad?" Andy asked later that night. It felt like it was after midnight, but it was only a little after ten. He and his father were preparing for bed – one bed. They would obviously have to share it. Still, it was better than sharing that wooden platform downstairs.

Their room was on the second floor. Apart from the bed, it contained a small table, a bedside lamp with a twenty-five-watt bulb, an overhead fan, and a rail on which to hang their clothes. They had stacked other clothes in their smaller bags, while the suitcases were stored upstairs, under the roof.

Outside, the street was dark and quiet, a surprise after the clamor of the day. Vietnamese go to bed early, his father had said.

"Wrong about what?"

"Giving all the pens to Minh," Andy said.

"Not wrong, just not custom. There are rules about who gets what."

"There didn't seem to be any rules when everybody was fighting over the stuff we brought," Andy said.

"Rules at work, just the same. Maybe some people are a little more strong and get a little bit more or better, but everybody happy in the end."

"Minh was happy," Andy said. "And Indy. And Grandma." He wasn't so sure about the rest of the gang.

"Rice cooker big success. Worth lugging it all this way, hey?"

"Yeah. But those other presents, deodorants and pills and all that. Don't they have all that stuff here? On the way here I saw plenty of shops, so why was everybody so excited and knocking themselves out over some face cream?"

"Is true, many Western goods available in Hanoi now. Very, very different from when I live here. But most Vietnamese still can't afford to buy, Andy. These things we brought from Australia are luxuries. You know what average weekly wage in Hanoi is? Maybe fourteen dollars a week. Much less in the country."

That was about the price of a movie ticket at home.

"Dad," Andy said, "did you know the restaurant was going to be like that?"

"Like what?"

"You know, sort of small and scrappy and right on the street."

"Most eating places in Vietnam like this, Andy."

"But did you know the Phuong Nguyen was like that?" Andy persisted. His father, after all, had never seen the restaurant. He had left Hanoi before the family had acquired it. So his father's descriptions of the place must have come either from his imagination, or from family letters. *Someone* had been exaggerating.

"Things are never quite as you think they are going to be," his father said enigmatically. "Bedtime, I think, Andy. You get in first."

Andy got into the bed and moved as far as he could towards the wall. He hoped he wouldn't have to go to the bathroom in the night. He'd have to crawl over his father and then grope his way in the dark down to the ground floor, behind the kitchen. One toilet in one bathroom for all the people who lived in the house. You probably had to make a reservation.

If this was the best house in the street, as Auntie Mo had said, what could the others be like?

"Dad, why didn't we stay at a hotel?" he asked.

His father climbed into his side of the bed. "Everybody would be hurt and offended. Family home is for family. Parents, sisters, brother, nephews, nieces all live here. They the people we come here to see. Why would we leave them for hotel?"

"We'd have more room. And our own bathroom."

"We already have more space than anyone else in house,"

his father said, rather ineffectually punching the pillow, a solid block of foam rubber that failed to respond.

Lying squashed against the wall, Andy felt greedy and ungrateful. He changed the subject. "Where's Minh's mother?"

"In Saigon."

"Why doesn't Minh live with her?"

"She can't work at job if she has to look after a child."

"Where's Minh's dad?"

"I don't know. In Vung Tau, I think."

"Does he send money for Minh?"

"No. He has married again, has new family."

"Why hasn't Auntie Trieu married again?"

His father sighed. "She has a child and she is over thirty. Too old. Vietnamese men prefer to marry young women."

"Even the old ones?"

"Even the old ones, yes."

"That's not very fair," Andy said.

"Life is not fair," his father said.

Andy was doubly glad that he had given all the colored pens to Minh. She would really treasure them.

"All those presents must have cost heaps," he said, thinking not only of the presents but of the diamond ring and the gold watch. "Did we suddenly get a lot of money or something?"

"No more questions, okay? Let's get some sleep." His father turned over, away from Andy, and turned off the lamp.

He was avoiding the question, just like on the plane when

he'd avoided the question about his jewelry. Obviously it was something he wasn't keen to discuss. Which would be all right, Andy thought, if at home he wasn't continually being reminded that money didn't grow on trees and they couldn't afford luxuries. Especially not luxuries like diamond rings and gold watches. To his parents, any article of clothing that didn't come from a market stall or a chain store was a luxury; going to the movies on any day except Tightwad Tuesday was a luxury; having a dog was a luxury; going to a hairdresser was a luxury; buying books or renting videos instead of getting them free from the library was a luxury ... The list was long.

Andy fell asleep counting all the luxuries he wasn't allowed to have.

Curled up on her mat on the kitchen floor, Minh considered her good fortune. Obviously she hadn't been meant to get the entire box of pens. The look on Uncle Tuoc's face had told her that. It had been her cousin's idea, but what had moved him to do such a thing? Certainly not her behavior at the airport. If Auntie Mo had seen her sticking out her tongue she'd have been in real trouble. And it had nothing to do with any artistic ability of hers, despite what he'd said. Hien could draw, but she had no special talent, and even if she had, how would her Australian cousin know of it? Nobody in the family would dream of including any news of her in their letters to Australia. Perhaps it had been the gift-giving. She'd watched him closely and noticed his surprise at the usual squabbling over who got what. Well, he'd be used to that if he'd grown up here in Vietnam. Perhaps in Australia life was so good and everybody had so much that there was no need to fight for every little advantage.

Tham thi tham, Auntie Mo had warned her disapprovingly: Those who are greedy for everything risk losing everything. (She was a good one to talk!) But the pens were hers now and already her mind was calculating their value. She hugged the box close to her. Other eyes had been on them. She would have to act fast.

If Vietnamese people went to bed early, they also got up early. Very early.

Andy groaned and squinted in the half darkness. What was that racket? A blast of some terrible song … then a voice screeching … Did someone have their radio turned up very high? If so, it was a selfish way of waking up the neighborhood.

His father stirred. "I forget about the Hanoi alarm clock," he groaned.

"What is it?" Andy muttered.

"Loudspeakers in streets broadcasting news and public announcements."

"In the middle of the night?"

"Not middle of night. Must be about five-thirty."

Andy groaned. Had he ever in his life been awake at five-thirty in the morning? He didn't think so.

"Many people don't get newspapers, don't have radio," his father explained. "This is good way to reach them."

The loud and rapid flow of Vietnamese squawked on and on.

"What's she saying?" Andy asked. It sounded like something really important. Imminent invasion? War declared? Approaching cyclone?

His father cocked his head and listened for a moment. "Catfish production in Vinh Long is up twenty percent, contributing to export market ..."

Big deal, thought Andy. Really worth getting woken up to hear that.

"Department of Planning has approved construction of new vegetable oil refinery ..."

Even bigger deal. Breakfast radio in Hanoi had a long way to go.

"When I was a boy," his father said, "loudspeakers in morning used to urge everyone to get out and clean up street and shop fronts."

"I reckon I'd rather hear about catfish production," Andy said.

His father laughed. "Come on, we get dressed, go downstairs."

"What about the bathroom?" Andy asked. "Will we have to wait in line?"

"We will be last ones up, you see."

He was right. When they got downstairs the big metal security door to the street was open, and things inside and outside were bustling. The TV was on, the volume turned way up to better appreciate the cartoons. Auntie Mo, back from Hoan Kiem Lake in her exercise gear of blue nylon sweatpants, lavender knitted sweater, woolly hat and white tennis shoes, was bullying Indy – Andy had already stopped thinking of him as Hien – to pack his bag for school. Auntie Thuy was stacking plates. Grandma was negotiating a deal for rice and noodles with a couple of bicycle vendors, while another vendor, the back of his motorbike stacked high with dozens of cartons of eggs – Andy counted sixteen layers – awaited his turn.

"You want breakfast?" Auntie Mo enquired.

"*Pho?*" his father asked.

"Of course *pho*." She called out to Minh, who came running in from the back of the house, and sent her off down the street. She was back in less than a minute with two steaming plastic bowls, which she set down on one of the front tables.

"Ah!" his father exclaimed, sitting down, his eyes alight. "One of the world's greatest breakfasts. I look forward so much to this."

"What, *pho*?" Andy asked. It was only noodle soup, after all. *Pho bo* was beef; *pho ga*, chicken. He'd had it at home, but never for breakfast.

"*Pho* most popular dish in Vietnam," Auntie Mo said.

His father nodded. "Vietnam in a bowl. Poetry in a bowl!"

"Mrs. Van on corner makes very good *pho*," Auntie Mo said.

"What you eat for breakfast in Australia, Andy?" Indy asked.

"Cornflakes," Andy said, and Indy looked aggrieved, as if he too was being pressured into eating something he really didn't want.

"Try it, Anh," his father said, in a tone that Andy was beginning to recognize.

Reluctantly, he sat down. It was way too early to eat. He didn't feel hungry, nor was he keen on eating anything that had come from one of those unhygienic street corner stalls.

The aromatic vapor from the bowl curled up and around him, and suddenly he was starving. He picked up the china spoon and chopsticks. The spicy broth was delicious, with chewy rice noodles and strips of succulent beef topped with chopped red chili, spring onions, coriander and mint, and lime chunks. It was salty and sweet and sour and bitter all at the same time, and ought to have been about the last thing you'd want first thing in the morning.

But if the idea was to give you a jump start to the day, *pho* certainly did the job. No noodle soup at home tasted remotely like it.

"Not bad," he admitted between slurps. There was no eating *pho* politely, you had to slurp. His father was already finished.

Minh giggled, either at his slurping or the fact that the

noodles kept slipping off his chopsticks. But it earned her a clip around the ear from Auntie Mo.

"Must eat *pho* fast," Auntie Mo said to Andy. "Take too long, noodles get full of water, get too soft. You like bread, cheese?" Crisp golden baguettes still warm from the oven, foil wrapped triangles of cream cheese, and small sweet bananas were pushed towards them. This was all right, Andy decided. He could forgo cornflakes for a few weeks. He smothered a baguette with cheese and started to eat. From across the room, Minh watched his every mouthful. What was so interesting? Did foreigners eat differently or something?

"*Ca phe?*" Auntie Mo set a glass in front of his father. Resting on the top was a small aluminum cup with a lid, and from it dark liquid with a rich aroma of chocolate dripped slowly into the glass and onto a thick layer of sweet condensed milk. His father, smiling in anticipation, lifted the lid and showed Andy the ground coffee inside. "We can thank the French for breakfast," he said.

"The French? Why?" Andy asked.

"Coffee, bread, cheese, croissants … all from French. They ruled Vietnam for seventy years, you know."

"But people still eat *pho* for breakfast."

His father nodded. "Every Vietnamese eat *pho* for breakfast, rich or poor, French or not French." He finished his coffee. Then suddenly he announced to everybody in the room, as if the discussion about food had reminded him, "Anh doesn't believe this is a restaurant."

They all looked at Andy. Auntie Mo, who was clearing the table, cried, "Ha!" Auntie Thuy stopped stacking plates. Indy grinned. Grandma cackled, gestured to the rice and eggs, and said, "Why does he think I buy all this food then? Why does he think I go to the market every morning? Just to feed these lazy-bones?" She scowled at Minh as she spoke.

Andy, embarrassed and annoyed, tried to explain. "It's not much like restaurants at home, that's all I meant."

"Restaurants in Australia rich and fancy," sniffed Auntie Mo. "Here, food more important than rich and fancy."

"Australians eat McDonald's hamburgers and KFC out of cardboard boxes," said Indy authoritatively. A wistful look crossed his face.

"You come with me to market, Anh," said his grandmother. "You learn about our business."

"Good idea," said Andy's father jovially. Andy didn't think it was a good idea at all, but he had little say in the matter. Indy, dressed in blue pants and a white shirt, was off to school, his father wanted to discuss family business with Grandpa, Uncle Hop had left for work, and everyone else was engaged in preparing for the lunchtime trade. Minh, it seemed, would also be coming.

Grandma pushed them into the street with a stream of rapid Vietnamese of which Andy understood only a few words, "Hurry, late, best food gone."

As it was not yet seven o'clock, he thought this was probably a wild exaggeration, and indeed when they reached

47

the small street market it was not crowded. Only a few people wandered around the stalls, peering intently at the produce, turning over vegetables, prodding the fish.

"See, we're not late," Andy said, but his grandmother now had eyes and ears for nothing but the shopping task at hand. She darted ahead, picking through the offerings on the stalls like a sharp-eyed bargain hunter at the after-Christmas sales.

"Yes, late," said Minh unexpectedly. She had not talked at all during the ten-minute walk through the relatively quiet streets. "These people here now restaurant and eating shop owners, like us. Ordinary people come later. Grandma not happy if she miss most fresh, best food."

Andy looked at her in surprise. It was the most he had heard her utter, and her English was very good – better, in fact, than that of any other family member. Where had she learned it? She evidently didn't go to school. He opened his mouth to ask, but before he could get the words out Minh said, "Your fault. Too much breakfast."

Stung, Andy could think of nothing to say. What was *too much* breakfast? He'd eaten everything that was offered. Had he taken too long? Was that what she meant?

"I'm not used to noodles for breakfast," he said lamely. "And I didn't know you had to eat them fast. Australian noodles must be different."

Minh snorted. "I think I call you Noodles," she said. "Aussie Noodles."

"No, don't," Andy said crossly. "My name's Andrew."

"Noodles better."

"Then I'm calling you Cheeky."

"Chicky? What, like those?" Minh pointed to where a bunch of squatting women were shaving the skins of plucked chickens with razor blades.

"Not chicky, *cheeky*. It means someone who's kind of rude." He stared at the market women in horrible fascination. Plucking he knew about, but shaving?

"Ha! You think I rude because I make face at you in airport? I did because you stare at me like this." She narrowed her eyes and frowned fiercely.

"I didn't!"

"Yes. You look to back of crowd to see who is most unimportant member of family."

"If I thought that, why did I give you the box of pens?" Andy demanded.

"Maybe you feel sorry for me."

Well, yes, he had, but Andy was feeling less and less sorry for her as time went on.

"Your father rich man now, but only because he Viet Kieu," Minh said. "If he stay in Vietnam he be same now as rest of family."

"My father's not rich," Andy said.

"Yes, he rich. He have important job in Australia, big house. He wear gold, diamonds, nice watch, new suit. Bring lots of presents, money. He very rich."

Before Andy could tell her how wrong she was, Grandma

was back and thrusting plastic shopping bags bulging with herbs, salad greens, onions, and unfamiliar vegetables into their hands. "Come," she urged. "Meat, fish. Hurry."

Off she scuttled, down to the opposite end of the market, Minh and Andy trailing in her wake. For an old lady she moved pretty fast, and she knew exactly what she wanted. Andy couldn't look at the cages of quaking rabbits and squawking chickens that seemed to know they were destined for the cooking pot. He turned away, only to come face to face with raw intestines and bloody carcasses hanging from hooks – so different from the styrofoam trays wrapped in plastic wrap and laid out in orderly rows in the supermarket back home. He watched in astonishment as his grandmother seized a cleaver and started carving up a side of beef. Expertly, she trimmed away the bones and thick yellow fat from the cuts she wanted and then turned her attention to a slab of pork. *Whack! Whack!* Andy flinched with every blow, but the meat-seller watched calmly, then weighed what she gave him, and wrapped it in newspaper. Well, why should you pay for what you couldn't use? Andy was surprised his grandmother didn't peel the rind from the melons and oranges before she bought them.

Now they were in the fish section and Andy had to concentrate on where he was walking because the ground was covered with metal basins full of live crabs and eels and small shrimps and buckets of – what were those huge pale-skinned things with the long legs tied together? Surely not …

"Frogs," said Minh. "You like frogs?"

He swallowed. "No." Especially not frogs as big as kittens.

"Taste very good," Minh said, looking at him out of the corner of her eye. "Also snails, and eel, fried scorpions. Dog, too."

Andy, appalled, decided not to look too closely at what was in the bags and parcels his grandmother handed him. She gave Minh far more to carry, he noticed, and he was about to redistribute the load more fairly when he changed his mind. Noodles, she'd called him. Just for that, Cheeky could carry all her bags.

Chapter 5

Andy had never thought much about what it would be like to run a restaurant, but TV made it seem pretty glamorous. Chefs in crisp white aprons and striped pants working in clean, shiny kitchens dribbled olive oil here and there, tossed pans of food over flames and prodded steaks on the grill. Relaxed diners sipped wine, savored each tasty mouthful and nodded in approval. You didn't even need a kitchen, you could set up your portable grill right on the beach. But no cooks he'd seen on TV had ever prepared a meal while squatting on a busy sidewalk. Yet there were his aunts, chopping herbs and slicing hundreds of spring onions into long green strips, their noses so close to the street that they were in danger of being knocked off by a passing cyclo or motorbike. They used double-edged razor blades too, just like the chicken shavers in the market. A small slip, a moment's inattention, and a finger could end up in the dish.

Or a long black hair. Nobody here wore caps or hairnets. Nobody stood at a bench or a cook top. Everybody here worked close to the floor, furiously slicing, chopping, stirring, mixing. Nobody opened a package or a jar or reached into a deep freeze. Everything was fresh and prepared by hand.

We should have brought Grandma one of those food processors, Andy thought, as he watched her expertly reduce piles of mushrooms to paper-thin slices. A dishwasher wouldn't be terrible, either. He noticed a woman he'd never seen before crouched on the cement under the stairs, washing pots and dishes in two plastic basins. Almost at her elbow, two girls supervised a cluster of hissing woks and boiling pots. Obviously, nobody gave a thought to *Occupational Health and Safety* rules. Back home, the Phương Nguyen would be shamed on *A Current Affair*.

Where were the men in the family? He seemed to be the sole representative. And he couldn't even cook. No matter. Grandma gave him a tiny plastic stool and started him shelling prawns.

My first day in Vietnam and I'm perched on a kiddie stool with a bucket of shellfish and surrounded by women. Good thing Dizzy and Hendo can't see me.

Minh worked as hard as anyone. Andy noticed that the sullen, closed expression she usually wore had vanished and she seemed absorbed in her work, occasionally even giggling at some remark.

When all the preparation had been done – by this time it was almost ten o'clock – Minh and Auntie Mo and Auntie Thuy and Grandma squatted in a circle on the floor. In front of them were dozens of bowls and basins filled with meat, fish, mushrooms, spices, sauces, eggs, herbs and onions. "Now we make the dishes," Auntie Mo explained.

For the next hour or so the women hardly moved. Andy didn't know how they could squat for so long, their knees tucked up into their shoulders, their bottoms hovering a few inches above the floor. He scuttled back and forth, helping to bring in the various bowls of vegetables and greens and minced fish and chopped poultry from the street, and the circle of women mixed these with ingredients from the bowls, and stirred and wrapped and kneaded and threaded meat on wooden skewers, all without measuring, all without consulting any recipes. Eventually some thirty different dishes were assembled and stacked, one on top of another, on the open counter.

Good thinking, Andy thought critically. They could be further seasoned by the fumes and pollution of the street.

Who were they doing all this preparation for anyway? Was anyone likely to wander into this hole-in-the-wall place that had no chairs, no tables, and no printed menus? Where the only background music was the constant buzz from the TV and the roar of passing traffic? Where the aroma of herbs and frying spices had to compete with the smell of gas and exhaust?

He found out at noon, when the first of the lunchtime crowd began to stream in. For the next two hours there was hardly space or time to breathe. The small room and most of the sidewalk outside had been swept and cleared and set with the plastic tables and kiddie stools the Vietnamese liked to eat at – and eat quickly. This was *really* fast food: gobble and go.

Plates of food whizzed past his eyes – steamed crepes stuffed with minced pork, cold rolls, spring rolls, steamed dumplings, six different pork dishes, crispy noodles with meat, seafood and vegetables, salads topped with handfuls of fresh herbs, chicken glazed with honey, and some strange dishes that were probably best left unidentified. People bolted down their food as if they had something terribly urgent to do afterwards and were out the door – well, if there had been a door – in about twenty minutes. Then a new group of diners took their places. The workers at the woks and pots sent in a steady stream of new dishes. The woman washing up under the stairs hardly took her arms out of the water, and only moved from her position occasionally to refill her plastic bowls. Indy returned from school and was immediately assigned to clearing tables and serving drinks.

At the height of the lunchtime rush, Auntie Mo beckoned Andy over to the cash register where she was simultaneously welcoming and farewell-ing customers, checking dishes, adding up bills and taking money. She gestured to the crowded room, to the sidewalk tables, and to the counter where people lined up. "All regular customers," she said proudly. "Now you believe this real restaurant?"

Well, it was some sort of restaurant, Andy conceded, and obviously popular with the locals. He spotted Minh crouching next to the dishwasher, slurping down a bowl of rice and vegetables. Auntie Mo saw her too, and yelled at her to hurry, she'd be late for school.

Cheeky went to school? What, now?

"So crowded, have to have morning and afternoon classes," Auntie Mo explained. "Hien go in morning, Minh go now."

Five minutes later Minh pushed past him, dressed in the uniform of blue skirt and white blouse, and shouldering a backpack. "See ya, Noodles," she said under her breath, and disappeared into the busy street.

Just after one-thirty, when the place had almost emptied, it was the family's turn to eat. Andy's father and grandfather came down from the upper floor and they all crowded around one of the tables, with the rice cooker in the center. His grandmother patted it fondly. "This only for family rice," she said. The paying customers would have to make do with pot-cooked rice. Andy's dad winked at him.

Andy was hungry enough to overlook the lack of hygiene he'd just witnessed, and the fact that Auntie Mo was furiously puffing at a cigarette, and the fact that everybody casually dropped their scraps and bones on the floor. He wasn't so hungry, however, that he didn't want to know exactly what was in the various dishes in the middle of the table.

His grandmother nodded in approval. "It's good that Anh

takes an interest in food," she said.

Andy's interest stretched only as far as finding out if he was in danger of eating any of the disgusting things he'd learned about in the market. But everything seemed safe, and he filled his rice bowl. His grandmother carefully picked the choice pieces from the meat and fish and placed them in his bowl. She indicated the small bowls of dipping sauces and the bowls of herbs and spices, tiny red and green peppers, fish sauce and chili paste, then handed him chopsticks and showed him how to season his food. He wouldn't have bothered at home – soy sauce and ketchup were enough for him – but he was a bit nervous around his grandmother and so he dipped and garnished like everybody else around the table. The food was wonderful. Everything tasted delicious.

"Good food, good cooking," his father said. "Now you see why this place so popular. I didn't exaggerate, did I?"

Not about that, Andy conceded. But it was still a little local eating joint, not a swanky restaurant. There'd been a heap of exaggeration about that!

All the same, it must be making money. How many lunchtime customers had there been? Forty or fifty, Andy calculated. And what would the average bill be? He had no idea, but one bowl of crispy noodles with beef at the Saigon Palace was around twelve dollars, and the lunch crowd had eaten far more than that, sometimes as many as four or five dishes each.

Of course, things were cheaper here. Say twenty dollars

a head minimum. Fifty multiplied by twenty was … one thousand dollars! And he hadn't even counted drinks. Whew! Dinner was served from six to eight, so the restaurant was open twice a day, every day. That was fourteen thousand dollars gross a week! The little local eating joint was a gold mine.

He looked at his grandmother with new respect.

No, hang on, something was wrong. What had his father said last night? He cast his mind back. *You know what average weekly wage in Hanoi is? Maybe fourteen dollars a week.* So how could people possibly be spending twenty dollars on lunch? Even ten dollars would be more than half a week's salary.

It didn't add up.

After lunch, Andy and his father set out to explore some of Hanoi. Andy took his guide book. "No need for that," his father said. He tapped his head. "All up here."

Andy took it anyway and was glad he did, for as they soon discovered, a lot of whatever was "up here" was over twenty years out of date. As they negotiated the crowded streets of the Old Quarter, their stroll impeded by parked motorbikes, broken paving slabs, hawkers, cyclo riders waiting for passengers, mechanics at work, shoeshine boys, and everywhere people squatting to eat or cook or drink tea, his father stopped constantly, to exclaim, scratch his head, or stare around in confusion.

"This used to be Mr. Long's shop," he'd say. "What's this Happy Buddha Mini Hotel doing here?" Or he'd stand gazing at a row of shops selling embroidered linens and silk scarves and say, "Where did the fried onion stall go?"

Sensing their confusion, street vendors, mainly children, swooped down on them. "You buy map? Very good map, only thirty thousand dong, three dollar." "You buy chewing gum? Postcards?" Women lugging baskets of fruit and grain suspended from bamboo poles carried across their shoulders urged them to take photographs. They whipped off their conical straw hats and tried to place them on Andy's head. "Take photo, very cute," they urged.

"Don't you dare," Andy warned his father.

"Only two dollar."

Well, that settled it. Bad enough to look like a dork without having to pay for a permanent reminder.

Food seemed to trigger the strongest memories for his father. As he strolled around, his nose was constantly twitching in appreciation. When they came across a vendor cooking *bun cha*, grilled pork, over a small charcoal fire, he insisted they have some, even though they hadn't long finished lunch. "I used to eat this coming home from school," his father said, licking his lips. "Street cooking has a special flavor."

"Yeah, like dust and exhaust fumes," Andy said. He meant it as a joke, but his father answered seriously, "No, no, these streets very quiet back then. No tourists, no crazy traffic like now."

In one street that was really more like an alleyway, an old woman in black pajamas was squatting in the gutter over a plastic bowl of washing. A half-naked toddler sat on the ground, his fingers splashing in the scummy water. The woman looked up and saw them, and her wrinkled face broke into a black-toothed grin. "Nguyen Tuoc!" she squawked. "We heard you had returned. A Viet Kieu from the neighborhood come back home!" She flapped her hands and called loudly into the interior of the hovel behind her. "Come, come and meet our Viet Kieu!"

"Do you know her, Dad?" Andy asked.

"Not really. Maybe I knew her when I was a boy."

A crowd of old men in black pajamas and white undershirts, ragged children and thin, eager women quickly surrounded them. They chattered in excited voices and fired endless questions, only some of which Andy understood.

"Where do you live now? Do you have your own house with a garden and bathrooms? Do you have a car? What kind of car? Do other Viet Kieu live near you? Is this your only child? How old is he? How much money do you make? Did you bring presents? You see how poor we are? Do you have some money for us? How about a hundred dollars?"

Andy was taken aback. Who *were* these people that they should ask such personal questions and make such demands? The old woman gestured behind her and let loose a torrent of Vietnamese. Again, Andy caught the words "Viet Kieu."

"What's she saying, Dad?"

"She wants us to go inside her house to see how poor they are. She says life here very hard, especially for people who don't have relatives abroad. She asks us to help her because our family has successful business and motorbike and color TV."

Andy wondered what her reaction would be when she caught sight of the new rice cooker. He said, "We don't have to go inside her house, do we?" It looked dark and uninviting, and they would have to negotiate a mass of oily engine parts and a broken bicycle that partly blocked the entrance.

"No. I'll tell her we are on our way to visit relatives."

Good move. Let her know that if they *did* have any spare money – which he was sure they didn't after all that gift-giving yesterday – it would go to family members, not to these grasping, greedy strangers. But what was this? His father had taken out his wallet and extracted some bills. He murmured something and passed them to the old woman. She didn't look overjoyed, Andy noted. Obviously she'd hoped for much more. Well, she was lucky to get anything. He was sure his mother wouldn't have been so generous. *Money doesn't grow on trees, Andy.*

As he and his father retraced their steps, Andy said, "Maybe we'd better go to a neighborhood where they don't know you, Dad, or you might run out of money."

His father shrugged ruefully. "It was a bit hard to get out of that one. But you know, Andy, these people do have a very hard life. We are the lucky ones."

"I guess so." He certainly wouldn't want to live on these

crowded streets, with all the muck and the smells and the incessant noise, but he couldn't muster much sympathy for the people who did.

They negotiated the maze of streets, most of which had no sidewalks, so progress was difficult. Andy's attention would be caught by a man pedaling along with dozens of plastic bags of goldfish stacked on his ancient bicycle, and then by someone else transporting a full-size refrigerator on the back of his motorbike.

They stepped around a small group of feather duster merchants taking a break from business to share a cup of tea and found themselves in a wide avenue lined with shady banyan trees. At one end of this street was a huge cathedral. "St. Joseph's," his father said. "This used to be very French, very quiet part of town." Now it was lined with expensive boutiques, jewelry stores, art galleries and trendy eating places. Cyclos and taxis whizzed up and down; tourists dawdled along and gazed down from the balconies of the Paris Deli or sipped lattes at Cafe Moca. You could eat tapas at a Spanish bar or pizza at Pepperoni's. ("Pizza! In Hanoi!") His father gaped at the shops and the prices of everything, from ethnic jewelry to lacquerware. Andy found it all deeply boring, and he was tired of fending off street vendors.

"Can we go somewhere interesting?" he complained at last.

His father apologized. "It is silly, I know, but I expected Hanoi to be the same as when I left. But everything has changed or gone or been restored. Shall we go to the lake and have *kem*? Ice cream?"

Chapter 6

Getting to Hoan Kiem Lake involved crossing perhaps the most frightening stretch of road they'd had to negotiate. Ten lanes of motorcycles, bikes and cars whizzed around the circumference of the lake in a never-ending whirl, all of them using the horn rather than the brake when anything or anyone tried to get in their way. And, as usual, there were no signs, no lights, no cross walks, no road markings.

Andy's father hovered on the sidewalk, stepping forward recklessly and then jumping back as his nerve failed. Andy, intent on ice cream – he could see the outdoor cafes under the trees at the edge of the lake – thought they'd never get across the road with that sort of timid attitude. He watched how the locals did it.

"The trick is to step out, walk slowly and keep going," he

told his father. "If you walk steadily the traffic sort of weaves around you."

His father hesitated. "Just walk into it?"

An ancient woman in black trousers and slippers shuffled past them and without hesitation stepped off the sidewalk, her eyes fixed on her feet.

Andy seized his father's hand. "C'mon, we'll follow her."

Staring resolutely ahead and keeping so close to the old woman that Andy could smell the fish sauce she'd eaten with her lunch, they plowed into the speeding throng. It turned out to be not really speeding at all, but traveling at a pace slow enough to be able to anticipate their movements and, as Andy had foreseen, take evasive action. Even so, it was a scary transit. The old woman shuffled away without glancing at them.

"Whew!" His father looked shaken. "I think I might have a beer after that."

A skinny boy in a dirty T-shirt sidled up to them at the entrance to the cafe.

"You want buy postcards?"

"No," said Andy's father.

"Maybe later?"

"Maybe."

"I wait, you finish, I see you later."

They took a seat at a table near the long tiled terrace which overlooked the small island and pagoda that Andy had noticed the day before. The cafe was neatly elegant, with small wrought iron tables, comfortable chairs under umbrellas, and waiters in white jackets.

"Can we afford this?" Andy whispered. When his father had suggested ice cream, he'd assumed they'd buy cones and eat them on a park bench, as they would at home, not in an expensive cafe like this.

"Oh, I think so." His father passed him the menu. "What would you like?"

A *menu*. In English. This was a step up in dining. And the selection of ice creams … Andy's mouth watered. They ordered a beer and a triple fruit ice cream sundae. The waiter brought them on a silver tray, with glasses of iced water.

The cafe seemed popular with tourists, and Andy recognized Australian accents in the middle-aged group sitting at the next table. He listened to them as his father went to get one of the newspapers on a rack near the entrance.

It made a change from the constant chatter of Vietnamese at Phuong Nguyen.

"Barb and I shared a cyclo from the Hilton," said a woman in white cropped pants. "We paid fifty thousand dong, which seemed like a rip-off. And the bloke didn't seem to know where to go. We passed the same spot twice."

"Oh, the taxis are cheaper than those cyclos," said a man in shorts and long socks. "Only fifteen thousand dong to go to the water puppets."

"My driver wanted thirty thousand, but I knocked him down to twenty."

"You have to watch them," said a woman wearing lots of gold jewelry. "But you can't complain about the puppets. Good value for only forty thousand."

"Dinner afterwards was a bit ordinary, don't you think? But at least there was an English menu. I like to know what I'm eating."

"The potatoes were nice. Makes a change from noodles, but that's the only dish I feel safe ordering."

They all laughed, and Andy tuned out. A Japanese woman at the table on his other side caught his eye. She, too, was eating ice cream, and she lifted her spoon and nodded and smiled, as if to say, "Not bad, eh?" He smiled back politely.

In the narrow space between a nearby table and the terrace overlooking the lake, a man in blue overalls was using pink paint to touch up a cement lotus flower adorning a column. He worked with careful concentration, oblivious to the American woman who sat only inches from him talking on her mobile phone. "Tell me about the fire ... No! ... I *told* you! I told you. Of course I've got insurance, that's not the point ..."

His father returned with the newspaper and poured his beer. "Nice here, yes?"

"The ice cream's good. Is that French too?"

"American, I think. During the war Americans built lots of factories around the country so their soldiers could always have plenty of ice cream."

Andy wondered if Minh and Indy ever came to this cafe.

He finished his ice cream – certainly one of the best he'd ever tasted, a real luxury – and licked his spoon clean.

His father frowned at him.

"What?" said Andy. "People here throw bones and stuff on the floor when they're eating. They reach across the table in front of you and chew with their mouths open."

"Different customs. Anyway, you've been taught good manners."

"I'm going to the bathroom," Andy said. A place like this would have a *real* toilet. He should make use of it.

When he returned, his father was looking at the bill. "How much was it?" Andy asked. His father passed it across the table. Beer, 12,000 dong. Ice cream sundae, 15,000 dong.

"What's the exchange rate?"

"About eleven thousand to Australian dollar."

That meant their bill was … Andy gaped in genuine amazement. About two dollars Australian.

"How can it be so cheap?" he asked.

"Not cheap for local people," his father said. "You see many of them here? For that amount, you can feed a table of people at Phuong Nguyen."

"How much was the bowl of *pho* we had for breakfast?"

"Maybe twenty-five cents."

Andy did some rapid mental arithmetic. His estimate of the restaurant's daily takings had been way too high. Ten times too high. It was probably taking in less than two hundred dollars a day, not two thousand.

"Ready to go?" His father left some coins on the table. "Wages here very low," he explained.

Andy realized he hadn't even factored in wages. All those extra women helping with the washing and mixing and slicing and grinding and peeling had to be paid *something*. And, of course, the egg man and the noodle man had to be paid, and the meat and vegetable sellers at the market, and the fishmonger, and the supplier of the bottled drinks …

The kid in the dirty T-shirt was waiting for them outside the cafe.

"You buy postcard now."

"No thanks, we don't want any postcards," Andy's father said.

"You said you buy later."

"No, *you* said later. *I* said maybe."

"You no say maybe. You say *later*," the boy said aggressively.

Andy's father ignored him.

"You a liar! You buy postcard!" the boy said.

"Come, Andy."

"Liar! Viet Kieu liar!" the boy yelled after them.

Andy felt uncomfortable. How much would a postcard have cost? About five cents. His father had given the waiter ten times that. They could have bought one of the kid's postcards.

It was pleasant strolling the lakeside path, with the traffic noises barely a buzz and the late afternoon sun glancing through the trees. Young couples sat close together on benches and gazed at the water. Grandparents supervised small children, earnest students studied textbooks and women hawked baskets of bananas and diced pineapple.

They rounded the end of the lake by the post office and his father stopped. He gazed out across the tranquil water to the small island with its red painted bridge and pagoda.

"I come here many, many times as a boy," he told Andy. "This lake is very important, very special for all Hanoi people. When I left I was not sure I would ever see it again." His voice sounded funny, and Andy hoped he wasn't going to cry.

"Hoan Kiem means Lake of Restored Sword," his father went on, his voice stronger. "Comes from legend about an emperor and a magic sword that helped him drive Chinese out of Vietnam. One day, when he was fishing here, a giant golden tortoise snatched his sword and took it to bottom of lake."

"Why did he have the sword with him if he was fishing?" Andy asked.

His father frowned. "Don't know. But that's Thap Rua, Tortoise Tower, in middle of island. Where's the camera? I take photo of you."

"No, I'll take a photo of *you*."

The minute Andy took the camera from his backpack, he was surrounded by a group of eager children, tugging at his sleeves and demanding attention.

"Hello, where you going? You want guide?" a boy asked with a friendly smile.

"No thanks," Andy said. He had a guide – his dad.

"You want buy postcards?" Children flourished sets of linked cards in front of them like colorful banners.

Not more postcards! His father waved them away.

A skinny girl pulled Andy's sleeve. "Where you from? You Japanese?"

Andy was astonished. Did he look Japanese?

"Korean?"

Korean? Andy told her he was Australian. *Uc.*

The skinny girl looked skeptical. "You Viet Kieu," she said. "You buy postcards to send home. See, post office over there."

"It's for our school," said the boy with the winning smile. "We have no money."

"Yes, for our school," the others echoed.

Oh well. Andy gave in. It was a bit like the chocolate drives at his school. "How much?" he asked.

"You buy two set, twenty dollar," said the skinny girl.

Had he heard right? Twenty dollars for postcards? When he'd just paid less than a dollar fifty for a huge ice cream sundae at one of Hanoi's best cafes? They had to be kidding. Even back home postcards didn't cost half that.

His father laughed. "If I pay that much, I also would have no money."

The children stared at them with big eyes in suddenly sad faces. "You Viet Kieu," said the skinny girl. "You buy postcards, help our school."

Andy's guilt returned. He didn't want any postcards, but perhaps he should offer them something.

"Ignore them, Andy." His father continued on his way around the lake.

The children followed them. "For you, only ten dollar," said the boy, his smile now absent. "For our school. Help buy books."

"Dad?" murmured Andy.

"It's not for any school," his father said. "These kids all say that. They buy postcards for a few cents and then sell them to tourists who don't know any better for huge profit."

His father took a bill from his pocket and gave it to the boy. "Now go away, leave us alone," he said in Vietnamese. The children, sensing that no more was forthcoming, grinned agreeably and scampered off to accost other tourists.

His father reached for the camera. "Stand there, Andy," he said, pointing. "I get pagoda in background." Andy hated having his photo taken, especially by his father. He took forever to compose and focus, even with a digital camera.

"Don't those kids go to school?" he asked. Then he remembered what Auntie Mo had told him. "Maybe they go to morning school and sell postcards in the afternoon."

"Probably don't go to school at all," his father said, squinting into the viewfinder. "They're a big nuisance, the way they annoy tourists. I shouldn't have given them any money. Will only encourage them. Smile, Andy."

Andy sighed and shifted his gaze to the other side of the

street where at least a dozen street kids were trying to sell postcards and souvenirs to tourists entering and leaving the post office. He wondered if they were all as fluent in English as Smiling Boy and Skinny Girl. Where had they learned it if they didn't go to school?

Wait a minute! That girl standing by the steps, the one chatting up a couple of middle-aged tourists in matching powder blue tracksuits ...she looked amazingly like ... surely it couldn't be ... Minh? But she was at school. He must be mistaken.

"Andy, look at me! And how about a smile instead of frown?"

He turned his head to look at the camera and when he looked back again the girl had vanished.

Had it been Cheeky?

Chapter 7

Back at the Phuong Nguyen, the floor had been swept and a few tables and stools set out on the sidewalk in preparation for the evening shift. As usual, the TV was on, and Auntie Mo and his grandmother were watching Vietnamese opera. Even so, his grandmother's hands weren't idle. She was sharpening knives and cleavers. She smiled and waved one at Andy to indicate that he should come and sit next to her.

He sat down, keeping a wary eye on the blades.

His grandmother nodded at the television and started explaining the plot of the opera to him. Andy understood about one word in five, and hardly cared about the rest. The singing sounded like cats wailing.

"Is Minh home?" he asked.

Auntie Mo shrugged. "You go upstairs, see Hien."

Perhaps Minh wasn't home because she was still hanging around the post office. Nobody seemed particularly interested in her whereabouts.

Andy dodged the dishwasher under the stairs – had she ever left? – and climbed to the second floor. He opened the door to the room he shared with his father.

Indy was squatting on the floor, examining the contents of Andy's backpack with great interest.

"Hey!" said Andy, too surprised to say anything more.

"Can I have this?" Indy held up one of Andy's favorite Rip Curl T-shirts. He didn't seem in the least embarrassed.

"It's mine," Andy said, unnecessarily. After all, they both knew that. He went on, "Why do you want it? You've got T-shirts of your own."

"Not like this. Mine got side seams. This all one piece, and good design." He rubbed it against his cheek. "Nice, soft."

Andy wanted to snatch it out of his hands. He didn't want to give up his T-shirt, much less to someone who'd been pawing through his private stuff. What gave Indy the right to do that? This might be his house, but that was Andy's bag. Any minute now he'd say that Andy had so much and he, Indy, had so little. He was fed up with hearing that line. But what to say now, with Indy looking at him expectantly?

He remembered the postcard boy at the lake. "Maybe later," he said.

"When you leave, you give to me," Indy said.

"Maybe."

75

"Okay, I wait." Indy got to his feet. "You want to kick ball around?"

"Where?" Andy hadn't noticed any grass nearby, and the house certainly didn't have a backyard.

Indy shrugged. "On street. Plenty space."

"No thanks." Crossing the road had been trauma enough. Andy couldn't imagine playing on it.

"I ask my father take us on motorbike tour. I show you my school."

Andy had had enough sightseeing. "Maybe later," he said.

"Okay, later."

Indy wandered off and Andy shut the door behind him. He repacked his clothes and zipped up his bag. Perhaps he should padlock it, or would that look rude?

He frowned. Why was he concerned about appearing rude? Greed and bad manners surrounded him on all sides, at the airport, on the streets, and even here in his own family's home. Nobody did anything or offered anything without demanding a price, and an inflated price at that. The three-dollar map, for instance. Andy had later spotted identical ones on sale in a kiosk for a third of the price. His father must be fed up too. Every local who crossed their path seemed to demand money from him. Andy thought it had something to do with the gold watch and diamond ring. You might as well hold up a sign for the beggars and street vendors, *I'm rich, come and hassle me!* And being Viet Kieu conferred no advantages. If anything, it was worse than being an ordinary tourist because people expected more from you. *You have so much and we have so little.*

"What you doing, Noodles?"

Andy looked up. Minh had silently entered the room. Did nobody knock on doors here? He got to his feet. "Nothing."

"What you do today? Where you go?"

She was just faking an interest, Andy told himself. She really wanted to know whether he'd spotted her hanging around the post office. "Oh, 'round the Old Quarter, to the cathedral, had some ice cream at the lake," he said casually.

"Hoan Kiem?"

He nodded.

"You like lake?"

"It'd be nicer without all the people hassling you to buy stuff. Like all those pesky kids near the post office," Andy said.

"Yes, pesky kids," agreed Minh. "You know what they called? *Bui doi.*"

"What does that mean?"

Minh shrugged.

"How was school?" Andy asked, watching her closely.

She shrugged again. "Same-same."

"Didya use your new pens?"

"Yes, I take pens. Very good pens."

She was pretty cool. Andy began to doubt whether it had been her outside the post office. After all, there were plenty of girls on the streets in school uniform who looked almost exactly like Cheeky, especially from a distance.

77

Auntie Mo yelled up the stairs and Minh said, "Must help get dinner. I very important for Phuong Nguyen, you know."

"You work hard," Andy agreed.

"Yes, I good cook, too. Everybody come here for my *van may*."

Whatever that was. She sure had a high opinion of herself.

"I make you special *van may*, Noodles. You see."

What Andy really wanted right now was a hamburger and fries. Or a hot meat pie with tomato sauce. Had the French introduced meat pies to Vietnam?

Later that night, he asked his father.

"Meat pies?" his father asked incredulously. The customers had gone and the family were once again all crowded around a table, eating. Vietnamese spent a lot of their time eating, Andy was beginning to realize. "With all this fantastic food, you want a meat pie?"

"What is meat pie?" asked Auntie Mo, puffing on a cigarette between mouthfuls.

"Australian national dish," his father said, with a laugh. "Eat at football or on the street, out of a paper bag, with sauce."

"Like *bun cha*?"

No, Andy said, it wasn't anything like the grilled pork doused in fish sauce that people ate on the streets here. He tried to describe the pastry case like a little bowl, the squishy meat, the pastry lid, the way you had to bite carefully so the meat juice didn't scald your tongue and run down your chin and stain your shirt.

"Sound disgusting," said Auntie Mo, throwing her cigarette butt on the floor.

"Meat pie have noodles in it?" Minh asked.

"No! No noodles. It's a pie."

"No noodles, too bad. You have this instead." She slapped a dish on the table in front of him. During their meals, he noticed, Minh was the one who ran to and from the kitchen, bringing and removing dishes, serving everyone. He wondered when she ate. "*Van may*," she said.

"Means 'cloud in the sky,'" Andy's father said.

They looked like stuffed pancakes. Rich, fluffy, yellow and white pancakes made from duck eggs. Andy had watched them being made by the dozen earlier that day. His grandmother placed one on his plate before everybody else around the table dived on them. Was he supposed to eat it with chopsticks? Andy bit into his *van may*, conscious of Minh watching him intently. It was filled with a spicy meat mixture – pork, he thought – he *hoped* – and onions and other things he couldn't identify. Stuffing escaped from the pancake and dribbled down his chin and shirt.

Everybody laughed. "Like meat pie," chortled Uncle Hop.

Yeah, yeah. Very funny. "Not bad," Andy said.

Minh frowned. "Of course it not *bad*," she said sharply. "Is very *good*. Best *van may* in Hanoi."

Auntie Mo gave her a slap on her legs, and screeched at her to mind her manners and get back to the kitchen. Minh departed, a mutinous look on her small face.

79

Manners, thought Andy. Look who was talking! He was growing less and less fond of Auntie Mo as time went on.

He had seen her, Minh was sure of it. She might have guessed that they'd go walking around the lake on their first day here. All tourists did. Still, he hadn't said anything, and that could be a good sign. Or else he was biding his time, the way Auntie Mo did when she suspected Minh of some misdeed – taking an extra serving of noodles at lunchtime, or a soft drink from the fridge. Auntie Mo would sit on the information, adding it to Minh's other crimes and waiting for the time when an accusation would have the maximum impact. Was that what Noodles was doing? Or perhaps he really hadn't recognized her. In any case, she wasn't helping herself by snapping at him, the way she'd done just now, and earlier that day in the market. Why couldn't she keep her mouth closed? She should be sweet and polite, no matter how much he ate or what he said about her *van may*. After all, he had given her the box of pens, and maybe he had even more to give.

She filled the plastic bowls with hot water and began washing the stacks of dirty plates on the floor.

Chapter 8

Lurking just inside the entrance to the post office, Andy watched the street kids on the sidewalk outside. It was a good place from which to watch them because they never ventured inside – no doubt because some official would promptly kick them out again.

There was no sign of Cheeky. Perhaps she really had gone to school. When she'd set off after lunch with her bag, and in her school uniform, Andy had tried to follow her, but had lost her in the crowds on Hang Bo Street. He'd come to the post office where he'd first seen her – or thought he'd seen her. But it seemed now that he'd been mistaken.

Never mind. There was plenty to observe. Mrs. Gowdie would be proud of him. Yesterday he'd noticed that the street kids all seemed pretty fluent in English, but he'd been surprised that many of them could switch to French or even German if the situation arose. English, though, was the favored language, probably because most of the tourists were English-speaking.

There was a pattern to their soliciting, he noted. The kids seldom operated alone, but nearly always in small groups, and they were brilliant at their job. They'd sight their target – a couple of backpackers, say – and hone in, bombarding them with cheerful greetings and questions. "Where you from? Melbourne? You Aussie? *Uc*?" Big smiles and laughter. "You very beautiful. You look like Cameron Diaz." (Or Angelina Jolie. They knew all the big Hollywood stars.) After the flattery and chitchat came the soft sell. "You buy chewing gum/postcards/guide book? Very cheap." After the inevitable refusals, the sales strategies started. "Twenty dollar at shop. Me, only ten dollar." "You buy send home. Your boyfriend love you, this postcard." Then came the pleading. The older kids would ask for help for their school and the younger ones would plead hunger, either their own or their family's. This generally opened wallets, if they hadn't opened before. It was hard to resist a small, barefoot child who did indeed look half-starved.

Andy wondered how much the kids made. You'd only have to con one gullible tourist into paying ten dollars for a pack of postcards and you'd have more than most locals made in a week. Easy work, really.

He had almost decided to go when suddenly he caught

sight of Minh. Yes, it was Cheeky, sauntering along the sidewalk, the end of her neck scarf like a jaunty little red checkmark against her white blouse. So, he'd been right!

Andy drew back a little to make sure she wouldn't catch sight of him, but her attention wasn't on those inside the post office. She exchanged words with some of the other kids and looked around, her eyes rapidly assessing potential customers. They fastened on a middle-aged couple in matching white sneakers who were poised nervously on the other side of the road, obviously debating their chances of making it across in one piece.

In a flash, Minh had sprinted to their side across five lanes of traffic and was bombarding them with smiles and a line of fast chat that Andy could well imagine. The tourists smiled, shook their heads, pointed, and … Minh was now escorting them across the road! Well, that was enterprising. Andy had to hand it to Cheeky. Forget about offering to show them temples and pagodas. Most tourists just wanted to get across the road safely.

With her prey safely on the sidewalk, Minh was not about to let them escape. She rummaged in her bag. Andy wondered what she would be selling. Postcards? Chewing gum? His mouth fell open as he saw what she'd pulled from her bag.

The box of pens he'd given her!

Surely she wasn't going to … surely she wouldn't …

"Very good pens, you buy. You need pen write postcard home. Look, all colors. Only five dollar each."

It was all Andy could do to resist rushing forward and snatching the box from her hand. How dare she! What a nerve this girl had, selling off his present – the gift he'd so magnanimously given her – to tourists on the street!

The two in front of her were having a difficult time resisting. They were, after all, under some obligation, having allowed her to act as their escort. After a token spate of bargaining – five dollars a pen was clearly ridiculous – the man handed her some money and pocketed one of the pens. The couple vanished into the post office, passing within a whisker of Andy as they did so, but Minh's attention had switched to her next target, two tall young women in tank tops and cargo pants, toting backpacks.

They were friendly enough, answering all Minh's set questions and posing some of their own – "What's your name? What grade are you in at school?" – but they were harder nuts to crack when it came to parting with money. Still, Minh hung in there, not giving up and steadily proceeding through soft sell and flattery ("You look like Lara Croft") to the final appeal to help her school.

That was a good one, Andy thought, his anger still high. When, exactly, did Cheeky go to school?

"You buy pen, help us buy books," Minh pleaded. "Vietnamese schools very poor, not have money for books."

The girls caved in, each buying a pen.

Andy watched her sales technique for another ten minutes, during which time she divested herself of three more pens and pocketed a wad of bills. By then he'd had more than enough. He waited until she'd concluded business with a young French couple (*"Vous achetez une crayonne, madame, monsieur?"*) before stepping up behind her and grabbing her arm.

Minh yelped, and spun around. Her face relaxed. "Oh, you, Noodles. I scared it be police. Why you frighten me like that?"

"What are you doing here?" Andy asked.

"I sell pens, make money."

"I gave you those pens! They were a present."

"Yes. Now I sell them."

Her attitude infuriated Andy. It was as if she couldn't see that she'd done anything at all wrong. "I gave you those pens to draw with," he said sternly. "Not to sell on the street."

"I very bad artist," Minh admitted cheerfully. "Better to sell."

"You could use them in school. Why aren't you at school, anyway?"

"I need to make lots of money. Can't do that in school, can I?"

The old Cheeky Girl was back. Andy's first impulse was to grab what was left of the box of pens, go back to the Phuong Nguyen, and show his father how she'd treated their present.

He paused. No, he couldn't do that. That would be telling. Besides, he'd been the one to hand over the entire box to Minh. His father might very well laugh and say, "Well, Andy, you'll listen to me next time."

He hesitated, and in that moment Minh's expression changed. She grabbed his arm. "We go, quick! Police!"

Around them street kids were dispersing as rapidly as a flock of sparrows sensing the approach of a cat. Minh took off in the direction of Trang Tien Street, Andy having little choice but to pound along with her. Eventually she slowed her pace. "Is okay now. Maybe police, maybe not. But safer not to wait see."

"What would the police do?" Andy asked, breathing heavily.

"Depend. Sometime take kids to police station, sometime beat them very bad. Sometime send to correction place. Most time make them pay fine, or make owners pay fine."

"Owners? What do you mean, owners?" Andy noticed that she had said "them" rather than "us." Clearly, she didn't regard herself as one of the street kids.

"People who own kids, make them work for them," Minh said.

"Parents, you mean?"

"No, not parents. People in Hanoi go to country, buy kids from their parents. Pay maybe seventy, hundred dollar, tell parents they take care of kid, train him in good job. Parents poor, don't know anything, they never see son, daughter again. Owner has maybe ten kids working for him in Hanoi. Make big profit."

Andy stared at her, aghast. "That's like slavery," he said. "Why don't the police stop it?"

Minh shrugged. "Maybe don't care. Police make money too. Grab street kid, then make owner pay big fine, maybe twenty-five dollar."

"That's terrible."

"Yes, terrible," Minh echoed, her face and voice bland.

Andy was shocked and a little bewildered. Minh wasn't homeless or hungry. She hadn't been sold to a trafficker and forced to sell on the streets. So what was she doing flogging pens instead of going to school? *I need to make lots of money,* she'd said. Why?

"D'you feel like an ice cream?" he asked.

Minh looked surprised. "Ice cream? *Kem?*"

"Yeah, *kem.* It's pretty good here. I had some yesterday. There's this cafe on the lake..."

"Cafe cost too much."

"Nah, it was cheap." Andy stopped, remembering that "cheap" was a relative term. "Anyway, I've got some money. You choose the ice cream and I'll buy it. But in return, you have to tell me what you're up to."

"Up to? What mean?"

"Why you're selling pens. Is it a deal?"

"Deal?"

"Yeah. I buy ice cream, you tell me why you're selling those pens."

"You not tell Grandma, Auntie Mo?"

Andy shook his head.

"Okay, deal. I take you to nice cafe *kem.*"

There was no point, Minh reasoned, in taking him to the place on Trang Tien Street where the locals lined up on the sidewalk to buy ice cream on sticks for thirty cents. She could go there any time. Her cousin had money, so she'd take him to where all the rich people and tourists went: Fanny's, the best and most expensive ice cream place in Hanoi. There was little point, either, in telling him the sad stories of some of the street kids who hung around the post office. Anyone who could ask why the police didn't help them clearly knew next to nothing about life in Vietnam. He probably wouldn't believe her, anyway.

Chapter 9

They retraced their steps to the lakefront, and near the corner of Le Thai To Street Minh pointed. "There," she said.

Fanny's ice cream parlor was open to the street. There were chairs and wrought iron tables with tablecloths under ceiling fans, and a refrigerated counter fronting the sidewalk. A small crowd was gathered around the counter, trying to choose from dozens of different flavors of ice creams and sherbets. The place was busy, mostly with foreigners, and the menus on the tables and the counter were in English and French.

Andy turned to Minh. "What's good?" he asked.

"Don't know. Never been here before." Staring at the price list, Minh had a sudden fit of conscience. "You sure you want to pay? Vietnamese *kem* very cheap, you know, not like here."

"It's okay," Andy said. "Choose whatever you want."

There was almost too much choice. Peach, guava, longan and lychee, watermelon, pistachio, passion fruit, ginger and custard apple, mint and cinnamon, green dragon fruit, green tea, licorice … Licorice? And what was durian?

"I have chocolate," Minh announced. She slid a sideways glance at Andy. "And strawberry." Might as well go for two scoops now that she was here.

Andy was also a traditionalist when it came to ice cream. He ordered chocolate and coconut. And because he wanted to use the bathroom, he added, "In dishes, to eat here."

They sat down at a free table. Minh gazed around her, and giggled. "Tourists think I rich Hanoi schoolgirl."

Her eyes gleamed as their ice creams were served with silver spoons, in tall glasses decorated with scalloped wafers, slices of fruit and whipped cream. They were also given sealed plastic envelopes containing wet towels, and Minh showed him how to pop his open by slapping it between his palms. It burst open with a satisfying little bang. Around him, Andy could hear similar bangs. He wiped his hands. Fanny's was certainly a fine place. He was impressed.

Later, when his glass was almost emptied of ice cream and he was feeling even more impressed, he said, "Okay, Cheeky, tell me what the deal is with the pens."

"Deal?" Minh latched onto the word. "Is same deal or different deal?"

Andy couldn't be bothered to explain. "Same deal."

"That means I eat ice cream, now time to tell you about

pens? Okay."

Over the next ten minutes, in a mixture of English and Vietnamese, Minh's story came out. She had started skipping school when she turned twelve. (That was a surprise for Andy, who had assumed from her size that she was much younger.) After twelve, she assured him, there was no real need to go to school any longer, but it was better than staying home and slaving under Auntie Mo's eagle eye and harsh tongue. She enjoyed going to the market and liked preparing and cooking food, but she resented all the tedious chores she had to do each day. In the family, as Andy must have noticed, she was the lowest member, and therefore the one who got all the dirty cleaning jobs. She was the last one to eat, the last one to have any money spent on her. In any situation, she was the last one taken into consideration.

Minh saw Andy's face and shrugged philosophically. "Is custom here. I understand. But also understand that it up to me to help myself. Nobody else going to."

Consequently, she had begun skipping school and joining the street kids for a few hours every day in order to make some money.

"What, begging?" Andy asked. He could imagine what his father would think of that.

"No, not begging. Never beg. Always sell."

"What did you sell?" *Before my pens came along.*

Minh stuck out her chin. She had taken money from the restaurant – not an easy thing to do with Auntie Mo in charge of the cash register – and managed to pocket enough small change to buy two postcards. "Is not really stealing, I earn that money good." She had sold these on the street the next afternoon to a tourist for a massive five hundred percent profit, and was on her way. Each new transaction gave her enough profit to buy a new stock of postcards and chewing gum, and to put some money aside. As her English and sales technique improved, so did her profits. And the pens were helping, too – enormously.

"They much easier to sell than postcards. Everyone have postcards. Only me have pens like that." She told Andy how much her savings now totaled, a look of pride on her face. "I hide money in safe place at home. Otherwise, you know, people find and take."

Andy could guess who she meant by "people." "What are you saving up for?" he asked.

"To go Saigon be with my mother," Minh said.

"Oh," Andy said, feeling a little stupid. He'd been thinking of clothes, girl stuff. Of course Cheeky would miss her mother. "When did you last see her?"

"Forget. Long, long time ago when I small. Ticket Saigon–Hanoi cost lots of money and my mother work, no free time, no money. I understand. So I get money go to her." She looked at Andy, her face bland. "Maybe you can give me money for ticket? You rich boy, not so much for you."

Andy felt uncomfortable. He didn't know how much that would be, but it was sure to be more than the pocket money that was enabling him to buy occasional ice creams. And would he be held responsible if Minh took it and ran away? "I don't think I've got enough for a ticket to Saigon," he said.

"Maybe later?"

"Yeah, maybe later," he agreed.

Minh made it clear that once she made it to Saigon, she was staying. She had it all planned. Saigon was richer than Hanoi, with more tourists, and hence more opportunities to make money. Her mother had a job and now Minh was old enough to look after herself.

"But you can't spend your life selling pens on the street," Andy began, and then he stopped. What did he know? Maybe you could. Maybe people did – had to.

Minh shook her head. "No sell on streets. Very hard life, bad things happen. I get a good job in nice Saigon restaurant, one where tourists go."

Andy looked at her doubtfully. Did nice Saigon restaurants employ twelve-year-olds for anything other than kitchen labor? At least she'd be earning a salary, however menial, which was more than she was getting at the Phuong Nguyen.

But Minh had higher ambitions. She wanted to be a cook, she told Andy. She could cook many dishes already and she had a keen eye for the freshest produce in the markets, but there were a lot of things she didn't know and a lot of dishes she wanted to learn. A nice restaurant, like the ones recommended in Lonely Planet guides, where all the tourists went, that was where she wanted to work. And in time she wanted to have her own restaurant.

She gazed around her approvingly. "Fanny's serve only *kem* and snacks, but look how is popular. And you know why?"

"Great ice cream?" said Andy.

"Yes, but also because staff speak English and menu in English. Real tables, chairs, fans, all very clean. So tourists see and they say, hey, this pretty nice place, can read menu, can sit down, write postcard, eat great ice cream, use clean toilet, nobody cheat me on bill. They rather come place like this, pay more, than go Vietnamese place, pay little."

Andy was sure she was right. He remembered the tourists at the lakeside cafe yesterday, and his own anxieties over some of the strange dishes at the Phuong Nguyen. But the Phuong Nguyen, too, was very popular. He pointed this out to Minh.

"Yes, popular with locals," Minh said. "So not make much money. Only make big money if tourists come to restaurant. Come, I show you." She stood up.

"Show me what?" Andy said.

"Show you eating places that make money."

"Okay. But first I want to go to the bathroom."

"Ha!" Minh pulled a delighted face. "See, I right. Toilet very important for tourists."

The toilet, like the one at the lakeside cafe, wasn't all that flashy by Australian standards, but Andy's standards of hygiene and plumbing had undergone a significant revision downwards in the last forty-eight hours. He washed his hands, dried them on a tissue he happened to have in his pocket, and then deposited it in a small plastic receptacle which bore the message "We share happiness."

Minh was waiting for him on the sidewalk when he came out, and for the next half hour or so she led him around the streets of the Old Quarter, some of which Andy recognized from his walk with his father. He was beginning to get his bearings.

"Oh right, Moca Cafe," he said in Nha Tho Street. "I've been here."

"You see prices?" Minh pointed to the menu on the wall. "Look, *nem*, thirty thousand dong."

Andy didn't think a few dollars was too much for spring rolls, particularly when you got about ten of them per serving.

"At Phuong Nguyen, five thousand dong," Minh said.

"Hmm." They'd been good, too. He looked at some of the other dishes on the menu. BLT sandwich and fries, ham and cheese baguettes, hamburgers, pizza, crepes, spaghetti ... Was this what tourists really wanted to eat when they came to Vietnam?

"This is the kind of place you want to work in?" he asked Minh.

"Yes, maybe."

"Not many Vietnamese dishes on the menu."

"I show you other places."

He followed her down Nha Tho and into the maze of streets around Hang Bac and Hang Bo. Minh pointed out the menus of several small places with names like Red River Cafe, Smiling Cafe, Meeting Cafe, Darling Cafe. All offered the same dishes, with Vietnamese dishes seemingly restricted to salads, spring rolls, noodles and fried rice. The prices here were lower, but still much higher than at Phuong Nguyen. Andy peered inside one of the cafes. Loud music, lots of young people and backpackers. They wouldn't have much money, he thought.

The tourists yesterday at the lakeside cafe had been older. And richer. They stayed at the Hilton and took taxis. The Phuong Nguyen could do with a few customers like them, but he couldn't see Auntie Mo and Grandma serving up Western dishes.

I like to know what I'm eating. That was what the Australian tourist had said.

He took another look at the menu on the wall in front of him. "Steamed rice pancake with minced pork" he read. Well, that was just *banh cuon*, a dish served at every second street stall in Hanoi. And what were "Noodle soup with chicken" and "Crispy noodles with meat and vegetables" but ordinary dishes like *pho ca* and *mi xao*? They'd been sensational at the Phuong Nguyen.

"You hungry?" Minh asked, noting his interest.

"After that ice cream? You kidding?"

"Maybe they have that pie dish you like."

Andy laughed. "Nah, don't see meat pies on the menu. I guess you have to be Aussie to cook them."

"School out now, have to go back home," Minh said. "You not say anything, okay? We have deal?"

"Yeah," agreed Andy. An idea was forming in his mind.

Chapter 10

They'd been bothered by postcard sellers and shoeshine boys ever since the taxi had dropped them at the Temple of Literature. Andy decided it was time to speak up.

They paid for their tickets – as usual, there was one price for locals and another for foreigners, a policy that Andy considered totally unfair – and walked through the entrance gate into the first pavilion.

"Dad," Andy said, "you wouldn't get hassled so much if you didn't look like a tourist."

His father laughed. "Everybody here is a tourist. That's why hawkers and street kids hang around. This is one of the most famous places in Hanoi."

"Yeah, but – "

"Very ancient university, you know, Andy." He consulted

the guide book. "Built in 1070 and dedicated to Confucius. People come here to pray for good exam results."

With its five connecting courtyards, huge ponds and red roof pavilions, it didn't look like a university. The lawns were dotted with students copying details of the architecture into sketchpads, and Andy could see at least one group of school kids in their distinctive blue and white uniforms. Perhaps they'd come to pray for exam success.

"We are walking same path as royalty used," his father said, still reading from the guide book. "Students used those side paths."

"Dad, you shouldn't wear that watch and diamond ring when you're walking around," Andy said. "And you shouldn't keep tipping everyone."

"They will think I have money whatever I do," his father said. "Anyone who can afford to holiday in another country is obviously very rich. Besides, they know I am Viet Kieu."

"But you're not rich," Andy objected.

"Rich to them. And why else should I stay overseas, in Australia?"

"But Grandma and Auntie Mo and all the family go on about how rich we are, and they ought to know we're not," Andy said. "Okay, our house is better than theirs, and we've got a car and all that stuff, but we're not *rich*, are we?"

His father pointed to a row of stone tortoises that carried what looked like books on their shells. "Look, engraved there are names of all scholars who got doctorates at university here, starting 1442. Before Columbus discovered America, centuries before Australia was settled, Vietnam produced scholars. Stand there and I take a photo."

Grudgingly, Andy posed next to a stone tortoise, but he wasn't going to be sidetracked. And he wasn't interested in scholars. "You and Mum are always going on about money and how we can't afford stuff, and we don't live in a big house like Hendo's, and our car's older than I am, so we're not rich."

His father lowered the camera and looked at him in exasperation. "Anh, you want me to agree with you, say we're not rich? Okay, we are not rich. Satisfied?"

"How did we get the money for this holiday then?" Andy persisted. "Why did Auntie Mo say that they have the best house in the street because of us? Why do they think you're a businessman? And how come you're suddenly wearing suits and expensive jewelry? Where did the money come from for all that if we're not rich?"

"This is none of your business, Anh," his father said.

"I reckon it is. Everyone thinks you're rich, so they think I'm rich too. Indy wants me to give him my best T-shirt. Minh asked me to pay for her ticket to Saigon." Oops, he hadn't meant to say that.

"Minh wants to go to Saigon?" His father frowned. "What has she been saying to you?"

"Nothing. I think she just misses her mother."

"She has no business asking you for money."

"I don't see why not. Practically everybody else in Hanoi

does. And why shouldn't she get a share, if you've been sending money here? You have, haven't you?"

His father sighed. There was a trapped look on his face.

"*Tell* me," Andy said. "I'm old enough to know."

"I guess you are. And you will keep at me until I do." His father looked at his watch. "Okay, we sightsee for a while, take some photos, then we go for lunch and I will try to explain."

After half an hour or so, when Andy had had quite enough of temples and tortoises, they walked back through the courtyards with their quiet pools and emerged into the usual noise and chaos of the streets. His father waved away the mob of motorbike and cyclo drivers who descended on them, and pointed across Van Mieu Street to a cafe. "Shall we go there? It looks nice."

It was called Koto, and it seemed many other tourists from the Temple of Literature had also discovered it, as well as a number of businessmen in shirtsleeves with mobile phones. Andy mentally checked off the plus points: an English menu, real tables and chairs, a neatly-dressed wait staff and overhead fans.

They sat at a table upstairs, next to a narrow balcony, and Andy looked at the menu. There was the expected range of Western dishes, but a good number of local ones too. *Chao tom*, sugarcane prawns – yum, he'd have that. And a pineapple smoothie. And maybe some cake. The young girl who took their order recommended the caramel apple tart.

At the next table, which was laden with bottles of beer and a variety of dishes, a backpacker was saying to his fellow travelers, "Vietnam sure makes you feel rich. Some cities, like London, can make you feel very, very poor. A parking space costs eight pounds an hour. That's like over twenty bucks, mate! Here, you feel very, very rich."

"Hear that?" Andy's father said, cocking his head.

Andy nodded. He'd felt the same way, dispensing presents and being able to afford deluxe ice cream in fancy cafes.

"I, too, feel rich in Vietnam," his father said. "Most tourists do. Prices are low because standard of living here is so low."

"I know. You said."

"So tourists can afford to be generous. But we both know that I'm not rich. I have good job, but by Australian standards I'm just ordinary worker, have bills, mortgage, car payments, Visa card debt."

Which must be getting bigger and bigger every day. Andy wondered where this conversation was going and how the gold watch and the diamond ring fit into the picture his father was drawing of an ordinary Aussie worker. "So why does everybody here think you're rich?" he asked. "Why do they call you a businessman? You're not a businessman. You work for the city. You're a gardener."

"I let them think I was rich," his father said. "It made them happy and it didn't hurt me. They think I am manager in charge of big department with many staff. I maybe wrote and told them things that were not quite true, little lies. So you see, in their eyes, I am rich, and they expect me to send money home, bring presents when I visit."

It was the first time Andy had heard a grownup (and his father, at that!) admit to telling lies. He couldn't help feeling a little appalled. "Why didn't you just tell them the truth?" he asked.

"I told you, to make them happy. You don't understand how it is with Viet Kieu. To come home without evidence of success would mean big loss of face – for them, and for me. It is important for us to make success of our life, and to show everybody that we have done well."

"Don't you think you've done well?" Andy felt confused. Anybody could see that the Nguyen family in Australia was better off than the Nguyen family in Hanoi. He remembered Minh's words. *If he stay in Vietnam, your father be same now as rest of family.* His father might be a gardener, but it was a good job that he enjoyed – wasn't he always telling them that the secret of a happy life was to be paid for what you enjoyed doing? And they had a house and a car and enough to eat, and he and Mai went to school all day and didn't have to sell things on the street for extra money.

"In Vietnam, people who work the land, who grow things, are peasants," his father said. "If I tell them I am a gardener, they would not understand. They would say, 'Why go all that way, risk such danger, to do something you can do back here?'"

"But it's not the same, is it?"

His father smiled. "Same-same but different. They exaggerate too, of course. Phuong Nguyen not quite as big and successful as they tell me in letters."

Ah ha! So his dad had been sucked in too.

Their meals arrived and his father said nothing more as they began to eat. Andy nibbled on his kebab, a sort of spicy prawn cake wrapped around a stick of sugarcane and grilled, while his mind whirled with all this new information. Was he also expected to maintain the fiction of prosperity? He'd already protested to Minh that his father wasn't a rich businessman, but now it appeared that he *was*, at least as far as the family was concerned. And if they were as rich as his father had been pretending to be, how could he refuse to give Minh the fare to Saigon?

"Do I have to lie too?" he asked.

His father frowned. "Is not really lying, just stretching truth a little, that's all. Remember Uncle Son, when he go back home last year?" Andy nodded. Uncle Son wasn't a real uncle, just a friend of the family who worked in the Saigon Palace. "When he go back to Vietnam," his father continued, "he take presents and tell family he owns restaurant, not that he work as waiter. Nobody want to hear that, means big loss of face. So little lie make everybody happy."

"But why doesn't he – why don't you – just explain how tough it is to be a refugee, when you don't speak English and you have to find a job and somewhere to live, and all that?" Andy had heard it from his parents many times. If they could explain it to him and Mai, why couldn't they explain it to their families in Vietnam?

"Very difficult for them to understand that everyone in

West is not rich and comfortable. And whatever hardships you have suffered, they have suffered more." His father finished his honey-roasted chicken and wiped his fingers. "Many people in this country call Viet Kieu 'lottery winners,' you know. We are the lucky ones who escaped to enjoy higher education and prosperous lives. They think we should return home and contribute to people's prosperity and strengthen the nation."

"What, come back here to live?"

"Yes. And set up businesses, help employ, educate people."

"You're not thinking of doing that, are you?" Andy asked, looking worried.

"What could I do, a gardener? No, I help by sending money back to family so they can buy house, establish restaurant."

"But that must have taken heaps of money."

"Yes, over the years, a lot."

No wonder they didn't have a flashy car and a swimming pool at home. No wonder his mother was always complaining about bills and the cost of living.

A thought struck him. "Does Mum send money to her family in Saigon?"

"Of course. Even a little bit helps." His father was watching his face. "You think we are wrong to help our families?"

"We're your family too," Andy said. "Me and Mai."

"You would rather all money be spent on you?" When Andy was silent, his father said, "What have you been deprived of ? Not education, not a roof over your head, not food in your stomach or clothes on your back."

Andy felt uncomfortable, and that made him a little cross. His father was changing the direction of the conversation. A flash of gold reminded him where it ought to be going. "So you wear that watch and the diamond ring to show everyone how successful you are?" he said. "And that's why you arrived in the new suit with all the presents?"

"Exactly. I am Viet Kieu. It's expected."

It was still a lie though. And something didn't add up. There was still a bit of the puzzle remaining. "But where did the money come from, to pay for it all?"

"Now that really is not your business. Eat up and forget it. It's not something for children to worry their heads about." His father smiled at the waitress as she delivered their desserts.

"You said back at the Temple that I was old enough to know," Andy reminded him. "The money's part of the story, isn't it? So where did it come from? Tell me."

His father sighed. "A moneylender."

"A bank, you mean? Someone in a bank?"

His father gave a short laugh. "You think banks give money to people like us? No, Vietnamese moneylenders, people from our community. I borrow money for new clothes and to come to Hanoi and bring presents. Uncle Son do same thing. He leave his car with moneylender for security." Seeing Andy's face, he added, "Don't worry, our car not worth all that much. And I give back the jewelry when we get home again. It is only rented."

Andy gaped. Who'd ever heard of rented jewelry? "But you'll have to pay the money back."

"Of course. Much, much more than I borrowed. Moneylenders are not generous people."

So they would be in debt, probably for a very long time. His mother would be complaining about bills for years and years to come.

His father looked gloomy, no doubt thinking the same thing.

"Don't worry, Dad," Andy said. "When I get a job I'll be able to help out."

His father smiled suddenly and patted his hand. "See, Andy. That is how it works. Lucky family members, ones with good education, good jobs, help others in family who are not so fortunate. Smart boy." He tucked into his apple tart.

When the waitress presented their bill she smiled shyly, said something in Vietnamese, and handed Andy's father an illustrated brochure.

"Koto: Know One Teach One" it read.

"What's that about?" Andy asked, as his father studied it.

"This is training restaurant," his father said. "Takes kids off the street and teaches them hospitality skills. All the staff here were once *bui doi*."

That was the expression Minh had used. "What's that mean, *bui doi*?" Andy asked.

"A name for street kids."

"Yeah, but what do the words mean?"

"Children of the dust," his father said. "Literally, *bui doi* means 'the dust of life.'"

Andy frowned. "Meaning that those kids ought to be swept off the streets, or that they're as unimportant as dust?"

"Either way, it is a sad name."

It was, Andy agreed. It made him angry, too. No child deserved to be described as dust. How could it possibly be a kid's fault if he or she had to live on the street? He looked again at the pretty girl who had served them. She was now tending to a customer at the front desk, and the boy next to her was mixing drinks like a professional bartender. "Did you know that people buy those kids to work for them?" he asked. "They go to poor villages and buy them from their parents. Then they make them beg and sell stuff on the streets and they keep the money for themselves."

His father looked at Andy in surprise. "Who told you that?"

"Why? Isn't it true?"

"For some of them, unfortunately, I think it is true. Who told you?"

"Minh."

"Ah, Minh." His father turned again to the brochure. "An Australian Viet Kieu started this place. I knew it couldn't have anything to do with government. So far it's trained over a hundred and twenty street kids. They live here, train here, work here and earn good salaries, then move on to jobs in top hotels and restaurants. Pretty impressive, eh, Andy?"

"They train kids to be cooks?"

"Cooks, yes. Also waiters, bar staff, front of house. Bill Clinton came here, look." He pushed the brochure across the table. "You know that saying about teaching a man to fish?"

"No."

"Give a poor man money and he buys fish for one day. Teach a poor man to fish and he has food all year round. You understand?"

Andy nodded. It really had nothing to do with fishing. It was about teaching people skills so they could be independent and support themselves. Like the street kids who would graduate from Koto.

His father reached for the bill and took out his wallet.

"You're going to leave a tip, though, aren't you?" Andy asked.

"I thought you not approve of me giving tips?"

Andy folded the brochure and put it in the pocket of his backpack. "I don't mind if you leave a really big tip this time, Dad," he said.

Chapter 11

What if? The two words kept echoing in Andy's mind. As the days passed, almost everything he did and saw reminded him that, as his father had said, he was one of the lottery winners. What if he'd been one of the losers?

Trying to imagine being one of the *bui doi* was too hard; he had no real idea of what their lives might be like. But every day he glimpsed what *his* life would have been like if his father had stayed in Hanoi all those years ago instead of risking his future in that rusty fishing boat. If Auntie Mo had sailed in the boat instead of his father (and he could just imagine her, bossing the captain and slapping down pirates), his and Indy's lives would have been virtually swapped. It was a sobering thought, especially when he got up in the night to go to the bathroom, and saw Indy and Minh and another cousin curled up asleep on mats laid out on the floor of the restaurant, Indy's face only inches from the front wheel of Uncle Hop's old motorbike.

When he and Indy kicked a soccer ball in the street in the evening, always alert for bicycles without headlights and scooters that sputtered around corners without warning, Andy thought of his school soccer team and the district cricket club he belonged to. Here, there seemed to be little organized sports – where would you play? – and no public pools to swim in, and if you wanted exercise you got up at the crack of dawn and joined the energetic crowds around Hoan Kiem Lake.

True to her word, Auntie Mo had dragged Andy along to the lake one morning, and he'd almost died of embarrassment when the ladies in her group had thrust a large red fan into his hand, slapped a white baseball cap just like theirs on his head, and insisted he join their dance class. The music from their ancient stereo was loud and crackly, and had to compete with a ghetto blaster pumping out a cover version of a Kylie Minogue hit for an enormous aerobics class nearby. Across the road, almost under the portico of the ANZ Bank, about twenty stripped-to-the-waist young men strained on bench presses and hoisted weights and barbells in their mobile gym, while old men in undershirts and pajama pants did gentle tai chi moves under the trees.

One morning he accompanied Indy to his school, a square, cement building on a patch of asphalt, and saw the plain, bare classroom where over fifty children sat in neat silent rows, four to each small wooden desk, sharing pencils and ancient textbooks, and repeating in slow, monotonous chants everything the teacher wrote on the blackboard. ("Just like when I went to school," his father said. "Same-same, no difference.") Classes started at seven-thirty, six days a week, and every class was taught in exactly the same way. The teachers were strict and there were many rules. There was no library or media center, no cafeteria, no gym, no track or sports field, no computers or science labs. Andy thought he would die of boredom in a Vietnamese school.

At home there was hardly time to be bored. When he wasn't at school, Indy was working – sweeping floors, washing stools, lugging empty bottles – or studying. When Andy saw him crouched over his homework in a dim corner of the restaurant, seemingly oblivious to the television blaring, people coming and going, and the noise of the street, he'd think of his own quiet bedroom at home in Australia, with his desk, his books and computer, and a refrigerator full of food in the kitchen if he wanted a snack. Most Vietnamese homes didn't have a fridge at all, his father said, and the one here contained only beer and soft drinks for the restaurant. Food was bought and consumed fresh every day, and there were never any leftovers. When all the food was gone, the Phuong Nguyen closed. If you wanted a snack, and you had money, you wandered down the street and bought a rice cake from a hawker, or a skewer of grilled meat from a woman cooking on the sidewalk. If you didn't have any money, you went hungry.

No wonder there were so few fat people around. If he lived here, Andy thought, he'd be as skinny as Indy and Minh. He would seldom go to the movies, and almost never to a live performance. His father had treated them all to a night at the famous Thang Long water puppet show in the theatre at the northern end of the lake, and the tickets cost so little, less than two dollars each, but Indy and Minh had never been before and were entranced by the music and fireworks and the puppets swimming and fishing and riding on dragons. Nor had they ever eaten pizza, even though a Hong Kong chain, Pepperoni's, had branches all over the Old Quarter, and there was one just a street away. (Oh, how he'd missed those delicious cheesy-doughy carbohydrates!) If he lived here, he wouldn't have the easy access to books that he had at home: no school library, no public library, few bookshops. It wasn't something he'd thought much about before – Andy was hardly a bookworm – but now that he'd finished the two paperbacks he'd brought with him (an Andy Griffiths and the latest Harry Potter) he missed having a book to read at night before he fell asleep. Indy had pounced on both these books with glee, even though he struggled with the English.

Yes, he was lucky that his father had chosen to leave Vietnam and that he, Andy, had been born in Australia. But surely that was all it was – luck. His father had said as much. "We are the lottery winners, Andy." He could feel grateful because of that, but there was no reason for him to feel guilty.

Minh, however, had a talent for making him feel guilty.

He'd told her about Koto as soon as they arrived home that day. She was up on the roof, taking down and folding the household laundry.

"See?" he said, holding out the brochure. "You don't have to go to Saigon. You can train to be a cook right here in Hanoi."

Minh flicked open the brochure and scanned the pictures of happy, uniform clad trainees. "What's this?" she asked, pointing. "It say 'sixteen to twenty-two.'"

"Oh," Andy said. He hadn't read that bit. "You have to be between sixteen and twenty-two to be a trainee," he admitted.

"No good for me then, Noodles. I not wait four more years. Too long." She handed back the brochure and unpegged a shirt. "You have a nice meal at this place? Food good?"

Yes, he said, the food had been very good.

"What you eat?"

He listed all the dishes.

"How much it cost?"

Andy couldn't remember all the prices. "Most dishes were about four or five dollars, I think."

"Each? Oooh-ee! You leave big tip?" When he nodded, she added, "I think this very good place to work. Make lot of money from tourists and Viet Kieu."

"Well, it's a non-profit restaurant – " he began, but Minh interrupted him.

"You got that money now?"

He was puzzled. "What money?"

"For my ticket to Saigon. You say maybe later you have money."

"Um, no, not that much money."

"You eat expensive restaurant meal, leave big tip, spend maybe fifteen dollars. Why you not give me fifteen dollars go see mother?"

"Well, it wasn't *my* money," Andy said, taken aback by her directness.

"Father money, your money, same-same."

"Look," Andy said, really uncomfortable now, "even if I had fifteen dollars to give you, I'd get into big trouble if you used it to run away to Saigon."

"Why?"

"What if something happened to you?"

"What would happen to me?"

"I don't know. Anything. You're only twelve."

"Twelve plenty grown up. I very good look after myself, you know. I do it long time."

Andy said nothing. What did he know of her life?

Minh piled articles of clothing in the plastic laundry basket. "Is good for me to see mother again and get job to help her. You think is good, yes?"

"Well, yeah." He felt he'd been backed into a corner. The best way out was to change the subject. "Listen, I've been thinking about those restaurants we went to and how we could make the Phuong Nguyen earn some more money."

Minh went on folding the laundry and made no comment.

"You want to hear my idea?" he asked.

"Is not your restaurant, Noodles. Why you care?"

Why did he care? Good question. Mainly, of course, because if the restaurant brought in more income, his father wouldn't have to send as much money from Australia. After this trip he was going to have a lot of debt, and he certainly wouldn't want to lose face by explaining to the family why he was unable to send them as much as previously. He'd continue as usual, and the debt would get bigger and bigger. Besides, it was poor business practice for everyone to work so hard and for such long hours for so little return. Grandma and Auntie Mo had obviously been doing the same thing for so many years that they couldn't see how they might make a few changes to attract customers with real money. Not big things that would require a lot of work and capital, but little things that he, Andy, could help them with. Sometimes it took a fresh pair of eyes to see how things were and how they might be improved.

He attempted to explain this to Minh, who didn't show a great deal of enthusiasm.

"Don't you want tourists to come to the Phuong Nguyen?" he asked, a little peeved.

She shrugged. "How it help me? Just more work, I think."

"Well, you'd get tips, for one thing. Tourists usually leave tips, don't they?"

She looked a little more interested.

"They pay more, too, so you could put the prices up. And

you could cook some new dishes, the sort that tourists like."

She giggled. "Like meat pie."

"If you want to be a chef one day, you have to practice and keep trying out new dishes." Andy was pretty sure he'd heard someone – Jamie Oliver? – say that on TV. He went on, "You'd be very important, of course, because you speak English better than anyone else in the family. They'd really need you around. Nobody would make you go to school. You wouldn't have to sell stuff on the street."

"Yes, they would need me," she said thoughtfully.

"They'd need you so much," Andy said, "that I reckon they'd have to start paying you a salary."

"Celery?"

"Pay you for your work. You could earn the money to go to Saigon in no time."

Minh shook her head. "Grandma, Auntie Mo, pay me? They will never pay me, Noodles. They say, this family restaurant, nobody get paid for working in family restaurant."

Andy thought there was a good case for arguing that if you weren't treated as an equal member of the family you should be paid for your work, just as the dishwasher was, and the women who helped prepare the vegetables. He was sure his father would agree. "I'll speak to them," he promised Minh. "If you do special work, you should get special treatment."

Minh nodded. It was clear these were her sentiments too. "How we get tourists come here, Noodles? You have ideas?"

117

Andy certainly did. He'd been thinking about his idea for some time. He dragged up a couple of the little plastic stools that were stored on the rooftop, and gestured for Minh to sit down. "Number one," he said, "we have to have a menu in English. Tourists don't know what to order, and they like to know what they're eating, so the menu should explain what's in each dish. The menu has to list prices, too. Tourists get nervous if they don't know how much things cost. They worry about getting ripped off."

"Ripped off?"

"Cheated."

"Ah. Pay too much."

"I thought we could do that together – draw up a new menu, with prices and explanations."

Minh nodded. "We use my pens."

"Number two, tourists don't like these little plastic kiddie stools." Andy indicated the ones they were perched on. "Tourists are bigger than Vietnamese. They have longer legs." He pointed to his own. "And they have bigger bottoms." He pointed again.

Minh giggled. "Bottoms!"

"And they don't want to eat on the street next to rubbish and parked motorbikes. We have to have a few tables inside with real chairs they can sit on." Andy hoped she was following all this. She was nodding as if she understood.

"How we get tourists here?" she asked. "Tourists look in Lonely Planet guide for eating places. Phuong Nguyen not in

Lonely Planet."

Not yet. He'd have to find out how you got listed. For the moment, though, they should concentrate on a less ambitious way of attracting new customers. "Well," he said, "this is what I thought we'd do."

Chapter 12

If you were looking for tourists, you could hardly do better than go to Hoan Kiem Lake and the streets surrounding it. They arrived in vast numbers every morning, to stroll and take photographs, to visit the temple, the post office or the ANZ Bank. They drank coffee at the lakeside cafes, and shopped at the shoe market in the northeast corner and at the art galleries and bookshops in the southeast corner. It was the perfect place to hand out their restaurant flyers, Andy decided. There was really no other choice, especially given the proximity of the Phuong Nguyen.

Ah, that was another thing. The name. "Phuong Nguyen" didn't exactly roll off a Western tongue. That was why, as he pointed out to Minh, all the tourist restaurants had names like Kangaroo Cafe and Love Planet. Not that he was suggesting anything as silly as Love Planet, but it would be good business to come up with something a little catchier than Phuong Nguyen. Even if it was their grandmother's name.

"Name, yes," Minh said, jiggling on her stool.

"Your idea, so we use your name."

"Andy's?" He considered it. Not bad, really.

"No, Noodles." Her cheek had a dimple Andy had never noticed before. "We call restaurant Noodles."

"Not Noodles!" He couldn't get her to stop using that silly nickname.

"Not Noodles! Yes, better name! People know then we have English food."

"But we don't," Andy objected. "Nearly all the dishes are Vietnamese. We'll just have a menu written in English. Anyway, I didn't mean 'Not Noodles' for a name."

"Why not? Very clever name."

"For one thing, we do serve noodles. Look at all the noodle dishes on our menu!"

"Take noodles off menu then."

"People like noodles."

"Okay, call restaurant Noodles."

Minh was beginning to look and sound a little exasperated, so Andy said quickly, because he needed her cooperation, "A restaurant called Noodles – people might think that's all we serve. And maybe it should be a bit more …"

He hesitated. A bit more what?

"More Australian." Minh nodded. "Like Kangaroo Cafe.

What about pie? Uncle Tuoc say pie is national dish. Many Australian tourists come if we say this is noodles and pies restaurant."

"But we don't serve pies."

"I learn to make. Anyway, is just a name. Kangaroo Cafe not serve kangaroos, I bet."

She had a point. "Noodle Pie," Andy said suddenly. "We'll call it that." He liked the mix of Vietnamese and Australian that the name suggested. Of course, there wasn't such a thing as a noodle pie, but there wasn't a love planet either, as far as he knew.

"Noodle Pie, good name," Minh said.

It was decided. Now came the hard part: writing an English menu and creating a flyer that would capture the attention of tourists.

"We do it now!" Minh exclaimed, leaping to her feet and seizing her laundry basket. "I take this downstairs, you get pen, paper." She stopped, and giggled. "Okay, I get pens."

"Should we go to my room?" Andy asked.

"Here on roof is best place. Nobody come here. This big secret, yes?"

Andy supposed it was, at least for the time being. He wasn't sure how his grandmother and Auntie Mo would react to the marketing of the Phuong Nguyen, but they'd certainly be more enthusiastic if Andy could first give them a practical demonstration that tourists meant more profit. He nodded, and they went downstairs together, Minh trying to hide her excitement and Andy's mind already bubbling with possible slogans for the new restaurant.

Noodle Pie, where East meets West ... Don't pass by Noodle Pie ... Why not try Noodle Pie?

The new name would go right at the top of the flyer, they decided later, as they spread sheets of paper out on the floor. "And underneath," Andy explained, "we put 'Phuong Nguyen,' and the address in Vietnamese, so if a tourist hands the flyer to a taxi or cyclo driver, they'll know where to come. We'll draw a little map, too."

"We need Indy," Minh said.

"Indy? Why?"

"Indy good at maps, good at all writing and drawing. He best one to do this." She flicked a finger at the paper. "Then we take to copy place, get lots of copies give to tourists at lake. Indy help there, too. Three people better than two."

Andy had no objection to making Indy part of the marketing team, although he was surprised to hear of his artistic talent. It flashed across his mind that this might have been at least one of the reasons people had been so shocked when he'd given the box of pens to Minh at the gift giving ceremony. But he had trickier things to think about. Like, how did you translate a menu when there wasn't an original menu to translate? The Phuong Nguyen didn't have a menu, had never had a menu. The regular customers didn't need one – they were happy with whatever was on offer each day. And that depended on what his grandmother bought at the market in the morning.

He looked at Minh helplessly. "So what do we write? We've got to give people some idea of what to expect."

There were regular dishes that were served each day, Minh said. Dumplings and spring rolls, of course, *banh cuon* and *nem*, and *com tay can* … ginger rice with mushrooms, chicken and sliced pork … oh, lots of dishes.

Andy wrote them all down. "Then I'll put, 'Ask for Daily Specials.'" He hoped that Minh would be around when the customers did ask.

"You can write special menu each morning," Minh said, "after we see what Grandma buys at market."

That seemed like a good idea. "Now, prices," Andy said.

Minh told him the price of each dish and Andy simply doubled it. "*Banh cuon*, eight thousand dong," she said, and Andy wrote down, "Rice pancake stuffed with pork, 16,000 dong." "*Bun bon am bo*, ten thousand dong," she said, and he wrote, "Spicy fried beef and noodles in fish sauce with garlic, onions and chili, 20,000 dong." It was still ridiculously cheap. Tourists could afford it. He added another ten percent to the prices.

"The dishes can be printed on the back of the flyer, sort of like a sample menu," he said. "On the front we have to have something catchy, something that'll make people read it." He thought for a moment, then took up his pen and wrote in large letters under the name of the restaurant, "Does Noodle Pie serve the best food in Hanoi? Many people think it does!" People like his father, Grandma, Auntie Mo, Uncle Hop …

"Put that President Clinton ate here," Minh suggested.

"But he didn't," Andy objected.

"Nobody know that for sure. How we know he eat at Koto?"

"Well, they do have a photo."

"Photo of him with staff, not photo of him eating."

Andy couldn't quite appreciate the distinction. It seemed to him that a famous person visiting your restaurant was publicity gold, whether they ate anything or not. But surely they did have to actually visit? "I'm not sure –" he began.

"Yes, maybe better put photo of famous Australian person."

"I don't think –"

"Who famous in Australia?"

"Well, there's the prime minister …"

Minh looked unimpressed. "Not as good as President Clinton eating at Noodle Pie."

She screwed up her face in thought. "Nicole Kidsmen!" she exclaimed suddenly.

"Nicole Kidman? The actress?"

"Yes, she very beautiful, very famous."

"We put on our flyer that Nicole Kidman ate here at Noodle Pie?"

"Yes, and that she say food very good. Best food in Hanoi, number one."

"But she's never been here," Andy protested.

Minh shrugged. "Maybe she been here and nobody notice."

Andy thought that was a bit unlikely. "Well, even if she did, she didn't say all those nice things about the food. If we say she did, that's a lie and she could sue us."

"What that mean, sue us?"

Andy explained as best he could.

Minh seemed mystified. "Why famous rich person care about little lie that not hurt anyone? We not say bad things about her."

Andy suddenly heard his father's voice in his head. *Is not really lying, just stretching truth a little.* "Well, maybe …" he said cautiously.

"I get nice photo of Nicole," Minh offered. She mentioned a shop just along the street that sold CDs and DVDs. Ky, the boy who worked there, would have dozens of movie covers with the famous actress and he would let her have one for sure. "We put her face here," Minh said, stabbing at the prototype flyer.

Andy decided to move on. "We should write something about the restaurant. You know, the food, the prices, the service, why people should come here." He bit the end of his pen and stared at the sheet of paper. How did you say all that?

"Say at Noodle Pie lots of delicious noodles with fresh vegetables, meat, fish on top, whatever you want. Big serves, little prices, nice friendly people. Not get ripped off. And big seats for big bottoms."

Andy opened his mouth to object, and then closed it again. That was it, actually. Minh had neatly summed up exactly what Noodle Pie was offering, although he wasn't convinced that Auntie Mo could accurately be described as either nice or friendly. On a good day, perhaps.

"Excellent," he said, causing Minh to glow with pride. "The best advertising is always simple. We'll put 'authentic atmosphere' too." He'd heard the phrase before, and it seemed to promise so much. Yet what did it really mean? In almost any Vietnamese restaurant, "authentic atmosphere" meant kiddie stools, food scraps on the floor, TV blasting away on the wall and motorbikes parked in the entrance. On all those counts, Noodle Pie could deliver. He wrote it down.

"We give this to Indy," Minh said, reaching for the sheet of paper. "He copy it, make look very number one."

Indy had indeed been good with a pen, as Minh had promised. It was his layout and lettering that adorned the Noodle Pie flyers they were at the lake to distribute. He had made only one mistake, and unfortunately Andy had not spotted it until after the copies had been run off. There it was, at the bottom of the flyer: "If you like our food, please email lonely plaint so that we can be listed." Would people realize that "lonely plaint" meant "Lonely Planet?" Surely they would. Anyway, it was too late now. At the top of the flyer Nicole Kidman flashed her famous smile. Andy had stuck her picture right next to the question, "Does Noodle Pie serve the best food in Hanoi? Many people think it does!" which cleverly managed to give the impression that she was one of those discerning people.

Andy looked around him, wondering where to start. They were at the northern end of the lake, not far from the water puppet theatre. The aerobic classes, weightlifters and exercise enthusiasts had long since gone and the first of the morning strollers and tourists were beginning to take their place.

He sat on a bench and divided the stack of flyers into three. The cost of printing them had taken almost all of his remaining money. "Here," he said, handing a pile each to Indy and Minh. "That's all there are, so be choosy who you give them to." His words were really directed at Indy. More than any of them, Minh would know exactly who to give them to. "Shall we start over there?" He pointed to the upscale Thuy Ta Cafe where tourists were sitting at tables overlooking the lake, sipping coffee and reading newspapers. In a few hours' time, Andy thought, they'd be looking for a place to have lunch. Why not Noodle Pie?

Minh gave a little snort and looked at him in exasperation. "You crazy, Noodles? Owner chase us away very quick smart. He want tourists spend money at his place, not our place."

"Oh. Right." Andy felt deflated, and a little foolish. He should have thought of that. He turned his attention to his other cousin in an attempt to regain some authority. "You all set, Indy? Remember what you have to say?"

Indy jiggled his flyers, a look of anticipation on his face. This was way more exciting than going to school. He recited aloud the words Andy had taught him, or at least the ones he could remember. "Want nice place eat? Noodle Pie very near, very good food. Please take fryer."

"*Flyer!*" Andy said. He tapped Indy's papers. "These are flyers."

"Ah, flyer. Like airplane." Indy made a motion with his hand, and Andy had a sudden vision of hundreds of paper planes made of Noodle Pie flyers soaring over Hoan Kiem Lake, some of them coming to land on the little red painted bridge, some of them landing on the smart tables at the Thuy Ta Cafe. Hmm, not a bad idea …

"First we go post office, then outside bank," Minh said decisively.

Andy stood up. "Just what I was going to say."

"Me too," said Indy.

They set off, following the path around the edge of the lake. Andy scanned everyone they passed, darting off to present flyers to likely looking customers. At first he'd been shy. "Umm, excuse me … I wonder … do you want … can I give you … ?" It hadn't been the most dynamic of approaches. Sometimes the people had walked on before he got around to the name of the restaurant. Others brushed him aside without looking at what he was holding out to them, or muttered, "No thanks, kid." Some were less polite.

"They think you *bui doi*," Minh said. "I try now."

She marched up to a couple of young women who were sitting on a bench and consulting a map. "Hello!" she said with a big smile. "Welcome Hanoi! You look for somewhere nice eat lunch?"

"Well, no –" began one of the young women – not unnaturally, Andy thought, since it wasn't yet nine o'clock.

"When you hungry, you come to Noodle Pie. Big serves, little prices, famous in Hanoi for delicious food." Minh thrust a flyer into her hands.

The girls looked at it. One of them pointed to the picture of Nicole Kidman. They giggled. "Noodle Pie!" They giggled again. "Is this your place?" one of them asked.

"Yes, family restaurant. See, food on back." Minh drew their attention to the menu.

"Where is it?"

Minh pointed to the map, and then across the lake. "Very near. You can walk. Or take cyclo."

"Okay, maybe we'll come," said one of the girls.

"You come, I take good care of you. No rip off." Minh waved, and strolled back to Andy and Indy. *You see*, her expression and body language said. *That's how it's done.*

The personal approach, right, he had it now. Andy tried again, this time targeting a backpacker couple heading for the post office. He hailed them with a cheerful greeting and then went straight into the direct sell. They were less impressed by Nicole but laughed at the name Noodle Pie and seemed taken with the menu. "Thanks, mate," said the man, who had a buzz cut and a tattoo of a snake around his upper arm. He put the flyer in the back pocket of his jeans, no doubt for easy reference come lunchtime. Andy's confidence soared.

The three of them split up, and in less than an hour they had distributed all their flyers. All they could do now was go back to the restaurant and wait.

Chapter 13

Aunty Mo frowned and let loose a stream of rapid Vietnamese as she set up her cashbox and register. What did they think they were doing with that table and chairs? A big waste of valuable space – four people, or even worse, two, spreading themselves around where six or eight stools could be squeezed in. Nephew Anh no doubt imagined he was back in Australia, Land of Big Empty Spaces and Long Lunches, but here business success was measured by number of bottoms on seats. Seats, not chairs, and Minh had been working long enough to appreciate that basic number one fact about running a busy neighborhood restaurant. They were crazy, the pair of them.

Andy knew what she was saying. It was remarkable how his Vietnamese had improved in the short time he'd been in Hanoi. "I've got a few friends coming," he explained, unfolding the last chair and putting it in place. "This table's for them. That's all right, isn't it, Auntie?"

Auntie Mo clearly hadn't expected this answer. "Guest friends or paying friends?" she asked suspiciously.

"Oh, paying friends," Andy reassured her. "They're staying in Hanoi for a few days. I told them this was a great place to eat and they said they might come." All more or less true, he reflected. If nobody came, he could say, "Oh well, they must have decided to go somewhere else."

"Humph! Friends!" Auntie Mo muttered under her breath as she and Grandma stacked the prepared dishes on the front counter. "If they don't come, what then, hey? We lose all that trade."

They *would* come, Andy told himself. All those flyers they'd given out – surely they'd score one or two customers? He looked across at Minh, who pulled a cheeky face and stuck out her tongue in the direction of the front counter.

"It's nice for Anh to invite his friends," Grandma said. She smiled at him. "These are school friends, Anh, from Australia?"

He was trying to think of an answer when a loud Australian voice called out, "This is the place all right. That's the kid over there. Hey mate!" A man waved to him from the street and then strolled into the restaurant. He had a tattoo of a snake on his upper arm. It was the backpacker from the post office. Trailing in his wake came his girlfriend, her jeans cut off above the knee and her hair braided and tied up with a red bandanna. Another man followed. He had long, soft hair and he wore a tank top and cargo pants. They headed for Andy and sat down at the table, dumping their backpacks on the floor. "We found ya!" the Snake Man said. "Thousands wouldn't have. Jeez, it's hot. Beers all around, I reckon, mate."

"Got Fosters?" asked the other man.

Andy looked at Minh.

"We bring you Bia Hanoi, very good, cheap," she said firmly, and sped off to the kitchen.

"No worries. Make 'em coldies."

That was the trick, Andy thought. Don't concern yourself with what you don't have, tell the customers what they're getting. He was conscious of Auntie Mo frowning at him from her position at the front counter and his grandmother hovering at his elbow, obviously waiting to be introduced to these friends of his. "Umm, this is my grandma," he said. He had no idea, of course, what their names were. "Grandma's the chef," he said.

"G'day, Grandma!" the Snake Man said cheerfully, leaping to his feet and shaking her hand. The others added their greetings.

"What's the house specialty?" the girl in the bandanna asked.

The other man said, "Noodles and pies, right?"

The three of them laughed. "We've just come from Haiphong and the food was terrible," said Snake Man. "We're starvin' for some good nosh, so bring it on!"

His grandmother, clearly confused, looked at Andy for clarification. "They're very hungry," he said in Vietnamese.

She nodded. Why else come to a restaurant?

"I bring them *nem*," she said, trotting off to the kitchen.

Andy whipped one of the menus he and Minh had drawn up from his pocket. "I'll let you look at this for a minute," he said.

"What's good?" asked the girl, as Minh returned with the beers on a tray.

"Everything," said Andy.

"'Specially my *vin may*. Best in Hanoi," said Minh, pointing to it on the menu.

"This is my cousin, Minh," said Andy quickly.

"She'll tell you about the daily specials." He'd just spotted two girls climbing out of a cyclo in the street outside, the Noodle Pie flyer clutched in the hand of the one wearing khaki shorts. He rushed to greet them.

"More school friends?" Auntie Mo enquired archly. "*Tay balo*, I think."

Andy couldn't see why backpackers couldn't also be friends. "We need more chairs," he said.

"Oh, we don't mind those cute little stools," said the other girl, who wore a miniskirt. She had an American accent. "We like totally respect your customs."

They took the table nearest the street, sitting on the plastic stools and spreading their bags and shopping around them. Instead of tucking their knees neatly under their chins as the Vietnamese did, they stretched out their legs – their very long, bare legs – straight in front of them, as if they were sunbathing on a beach. One even slipped off her flip flops.

Auntie Mo regarded them darkly. "Look at them, pointing the soles of their feet at other people! Barbarians!"

Andy tried to offer them a menu but they waved it away. "Can't we just point to what we want?"

"Sure," he said.

"It all looks delicious. And so fresh! We'll have that, and that. Oh, and some of *that*! We love Asian food! What have you got to drink? No, not Pepsi, something local."

Andy brought cans of Coco Juice and demonstrated how to shake them in order to mix up the solids that settled at the bottom. They inserted straws and took tentative sips.

"A bit syrupy," said Miniskirt.

"Smells like sweat," said the other. They both wrinkled their noses.

"I guess we'll have Pepsi," said Miniskirt.

Andy raced away to the fridge.

Auntie Mo intercepted him. "Tell your barbarian friends we don't serve *Asian* food," she sniffed. "We serve *Vietnamese* food."

"That's probably what they meant," Andy said.

A middle-aged couple was next to arrive. The man had a big stomach that hung over the belt of his neatly pressed trousers, and the woman's snug capri pants revealed a very generous rear end. Andy saw immediately that they weren't going to be happy about squatting on little stools. He looked around in panic, but Minh had already unfolded a small round table and set out chairs. The tourists sank into them with relief. "I believe I saw you today, young lady," the woman said, fanning herself with the Noodle Pie flyer.

Minh smiled. "Yes, me. Where you from?"

"We're from Sydney," the woman said.

"Oh, Nicole Kidman from Sydney too," Minh said brightly. "You want eat what Nicole Kidman eat?"

"Really?" said the woman. "I thought that was just a joke."

"No joke." Minh handed them a menu. "You start with shrimp dumplings and cold rolls, very nice, you like. Then I bring you salad and nice saucy meat."

They beamed at her. "That saucy meat sounds good!" the man said.

Minh certainly knew how to handle customers, Andy thought admiringly.

When the Phuong Nguyen regulars arrived, they found their favorite spots occupied by tourists. Some stepped politely over the backpacks, bags and shopping, ignored the bare legs, and squeezed in somehow. Others complained loudly, and extra tables and stools were set out on the street. They put their heads down, gobbled the food that was put in front of them with maximum speed, and left. The tourists chatted, discussed the menu choices with each other, sipped their drinks and looked around them as if they had all the time in the world.

Andy congratulated himself. The Noodle Pie marketing

campaign had certainly been successful, nobody could deny
that. The three backpackers were tucking into their noodles
and fried fish, the two girls were asking for napkins – *napkins!*
– and Minh was showing the Sydney couple how to eat
Vietnamese-style. Take some salad leaves, pile on fresh herbs,
plenty of mint and basil, maybe some chopped chili, pick up
a piece of meat with your chopsticks and place it in the center
of the leaves. Now wrap it all up, dip it into the sauce and eat
the roll with your fingers. "Delicious, and so fresh!" said the
Sydney lady. "Did Nicole do this?"

Some of the regular customers were now being turned
away. There simply wasn't room for them. Turning away
customers! Anyone could see that this hit Auntie Mo the
hardest. Even Grandma was looking worried. "You have so
many friends, Anh," she whispered to him. "And they all come
at the same time."

"Good for business, Grandma," he murmured back.

A newcomer, a lady wearing a floppy hat and clutching a
Noodle Pie flyer, was hovering around the entrance, looking
undecided. Before Andy could act, Minh flashed by and took
her by the hand, propelling her to the backpackers' table.
"You sit here," she said in that firm voice Andy was beginning
to recognize. "Nice people, not good you eat lonely."

"Cheers, love, what'll ya have?" Snake Tattoo said, pulling
out the spare chair.

"Do we have napkins?" Andy whispered to Minh.

"What?"

He mimicked washing his hands. "Tell them go bathroom," Minh said. Andy made a mental note to tell his grandmother about those hygienically sealed pop packets of wet towels that were so handy when you were eating with your fingers.

The girl in the khaki shorts returned from the bathroom and murmured to her companion, "They're washing up right outside, Jen. On the floor. In a plastic bucket."

"It's a totally different culture here, Kyra, remember."

Mrs. Sydney beckoned to Andy. "I don't like to be a nuisance," she said in an exaggerated whisper, "but I wonder if you could ask that lady at the counter to stop smoking."

Ask Auntie Mo to stop smoking? Andy quaked at the thought.

"I know it's not against the law here – goodness, the things people do in restaurants and trains! – but it's my husband, you see," Mrs. Sydney went on. "It irritates his sinuses."

"Stop fussing, Phyllis," Mr. Sydney said. "My sinuses can take a little smoke." He winked at Andy.

"Well, it's unhygienic, Mal."

"We're not in Point Piper now, Phyllis."

Andy looked from one to the other. Did they want him to do something or not?

At that moment Indy sauntered in from school, his eyes wide with amazement and glee.

"My Noodle Pie flyers big success!" he crowed to Andy. "This number one restaurant now. Soon be in Lonely Planet!"

Seeing him, Auntie Mo stubbed out her cigarette, thus neatly solving Andy's dilemma, and made a grab for her son's arm. "Another table and stools!" she ordered. "Put them out on the street before we lose more customers. Already some of my regulars have left."

"Put them where?" Indy asked. The area immediately in front of the restaurant was already full of customers.

"Clear away some of Mrs. Nam's stuff," Auntie Mo said briskly.

Mrs. Nam's shop next door sold decorative pottery and lacquerware, many of which were artistically displayed on the front steps and sidewalk, exactly where passersby would be most likely to step on a tray or knock over a teapot. Perhaps that was the idea. Only the other day Andy had seen one hapless tourist forced to buy a whole tea set because she'd done exactly that.

Indy shrugged and did as he was ordered. Within minutes Mrs. Nam had shot out of her shop and was loudly expressing her displeasure. Indy tried to explain, but Mrs. Nam was having none of it. She picked up a stool and threw it into the gutter. Auntie Mo shrieked, and ordered Indy to pick up the stool and put it back. Mrs. Nam grabbed another stool and said that if he did, she would throw the next stool at him. What exactly was her problem? Auntie Mo demanded. Look, her shop was empty, no customers at all, whereas the Phuong Nguyen was bursting at its seams. Common sense dictated that they should take more of the available sidewalk space.

It was not *available*, Mrs. Nam screeched indignantly. it was *her* space. It started *here*. She waved her arms, gesturing at the invisible line. And today, retorted Auntie Mo, it started *here*. She picked up a large decorated urn and moved it half a foot closer to the shop's entrance. Mrs. Nam, her eyes spitting fire, immediately moved it back again. *Stalemate.*

Andy sighed. This could go on all afternoon.

Traders in adjoining shops and businesses, attracted by the sounds of a good neighborhood squabble, wandered up to listen, joke and take sides. The Noodle Pie customers looked on with interest too. Mrs. Sydney pulled a digital camera out of her handbag. "You're right, Mal, we're certainly *not* in Point Piper!" she exclaimed, snapping away as another stool went flying, narrowly missing a cyclo driver who happened to be passing. Enraged, he jumped off his bike and added his high-pitched protests to the babble.

Chapter 14

Andy saw their chances of making the next edition of Lonely Planet slipping away. He looked around for his grandmother. "Grandma, do something!" he implored.

The old lady, clucking her tongue, grabbed a twig broom from behind the counter and entered the fray. What exactly was she planning to do with a broom? Andy asked himself, beat Mrs. Nam into submission?

"Onya, Grandma!" Snake Man called out.

Just at that moment Andy's father and grandfather, who had been visiting old family friends, alighted from a taxi at the end of the street. Andy could see the surprise on their faces as they took in the small drama taking place in front of the Phuong Nguyen.

They hurried up. "What's going on here?" his father asked.

Andy tried to explain.

"What's Grandma doing with that broom?"

"I think she just grabbed the first weapon she saw," Andy said.

"Weapon!" He shook his head. "This is a silly quarrel that has gone too far."

"Ah, the Viet Kieu!" exclaimed Mrs. Nam, spotting him. "You who have so much now try to claim even more!" She appealed to the circle of onlookers. "A rich Viet Kieu tries to drive a poor woman out of business, what do you think of that?"

Andy thought that was a gross exaggeration on every count, especially since his father hadn't even been present, but his father bowed and said, "Forgive my family, Mrs. Nam. They should have respected the boundaries and asked your permission. The sudden rush of business has gone to their heads. Please accept our apologies."

Mrs. Nam, who clearly hadn't expected such courtesies, stood her ground but seemed somewhat mollified. "My son and nephew will of course replace your goods that were moved," he added. Then, more quietly, "Please accept this for your lost business."

Peace was restored. The circle of onlookers drifted away.

"What a complaining woman," Auntie Mo muttered as they all went back inside.

Grandma shrugged. "*Duoc cai chay, thua cai coi.*" Some people will always complain.

"You shouldn't have given her any money, Younger Brother."

"Enough! You make the trouble and I have to sort it out."

"That's what I love about eating in Asia," proclaimed the backpacker girl in the bandanna. "So much street theatre."

"Never a dull moment," said Snake Man. He called for more beers.

"I liked some of that lacquerware she had," Mrs. Sydney said to her husband. "We might go next door and look at it afterwards. I wonder if there's a dessert menu?"

The two girls called for their bill. "Do you take American Express?"

"My back is killing me," Andy's grandfather said. "I think I'll go and lie down. Can someone bring me some tea, please? If everybody's not too busy."

"Come, come!" Grandma took his arm. "Minh! Tea!"

"I'm busy serving customers," Minh muttered, bringing in the beers.

Auntie Mo glared at her. "What impudence! Who do you think you are, miss?"

Minh wheeled around, her eyes flashing. "A cook, a good cook. Also someone who can speak to customers in English. That's why these tourists are here. Did you think they all found us just by accident?"

Auntie Mo was taken aback, and Andy, too, stared at his cousin in surprise. It was the first time he had seen Minh stand up to Auntie Mo.

"That's something I'd certainly like to hear more about," said Andy's father. He looked enquiringly at Minh.

Minh looked at Andy.

Where to begin? "Umm," said Andy, hesitating.

"Maybe the customers can tell us," his father said. He took the tray of beers from Minh's hands and went over to the backpackers' table. "G'day," he said. "I'm Tuoc Nguyen, one of the owners. I hope the food has been to your liking?"

"Too right," said Snake Man. The others nodded in agreement. "Beaut' little place you've got here, mate."

"Really authentic," said the girl.

"How did you hear about us?"

The lady in the floppy hat produced her Noodle Pie flyer. "Your children are great ambassadors," she chirruped. "They came up to me at the lake this morning and gave me this. I thought, well, why not? And I'm glad I did. Such a friendly place. And the food is superb."

"Yep," said the man with the long hair. "Next internet cafe I go to, I'm emailing 'Lonely Plaint' about Noodle Pie. Might leave out the recommendation from Nicole Kidman, but."

His companions laughed.

Andy's father was reading the flyer, his face a mix of surprise and bewilderment.

"Dad," said Andy, "I can explain."

"You come here quick and explain we don't take this credit card," Auntie Mo called to him from the front counter. "Cash," she was saying to the two girls.

"But it's like thousands! We don't have that much."

Andy joined them. "That's in dong," he explained. "Vietnamese money. It's, umm … about eight dollars."

"Really? Is that all? Here, keep the change. The service was really, really good." She handed Andy some money. "Thanks a lot. Seeya! Jen, let's check out the shop next door while we're here." With a wave, the two girls headed into Mrs. Nam's.

Andy looked at the bill in his hand. It was American, ten dollars. They had paid way too much. Just as he opened his mouth to call them back, the money was plucked from his hand. "I take that," said Auntie Mo.

"Some of it's a tip," said Andy.

Auntie Mo sniffed.

It was another half hour before all the lunchtime diners departed and the family could have their midday meal. But it was hours past midday – Andy's grandfather had fallen asleep in the meantime – and besides, there wasn't a great deal of food left. The kitchen was almost bare and the extra workers had been sent home. In any other restaurant in the world, Andy reflected, this would be a cause for rejoicing. In this one, it was the cause of grumbling.

"At least we can have rice," Grandma said, bringing out the electric rice cooker. Indy had been given some money and sent around the corner to where, luckily, the *bun cha* woman was still grilling her pork balls. "Imagine having to buy our lunch from the street!" Grandma clucked her tongue disapprovingly. "Those *tay balo* and their big stomachs!"

"I thought the foreigners were never going to leave," complained Auntie Mo. "They sit, they look, they chat. They take one hour, two hours, to eat meal."

"Not like Vietnamese," agreed Auntie Thuy. "They eat quick, then leave."

Everybody agreed that this was much more civilized and much better for business.

"We don't have room for chat-chat tourists," Grandma said. "We will lose our regular customers."

Andy was a bit put out. "But look at how much the tourists spent," he protested.

"And they left tips," Minh added, throwing a look in Auntie Mo's direction. "Vietnamese customers never leave tips."

"We might be in next Lonely Planet," Indy said hopefully.

Andy's father placed the Noodle Pie flyer in the center of the table. "I think it's time somebody explained what this is all about. Anh, this was your idea?"

Andy admitted that it was. "I just wanted to help the restaurant make some more money. I thought, you know, if it had an English name and menu and proper chairs, then tourists would come and spend money …" He hesitated. He didn't want to spell it out in front of the whole table. Didn't his father understand? "More money coming in," he emphasized. "That'd be a good thing, wouldn't it, Dad? Good for the family, and good for you," he added in an undertone.

His father looked at him. "Ah," he said softly.

Auntie Mo had swooped on the flyer and was examining it with deep interest. "Noodle Pie," she read out. "What is this funny name?"

"Noodle Pie!" Grandma cackled, showing all her teeth.

Auntie Thuy pointed to Nicole Kidman's photo. "She is famous actress, yes? Has she been here? I don't remember."

Now Auntie Mo had seen the prices. "*Oigioi oi!* All prices double, more than double! What have you done? Who would pay such prices!"

She took a swipe at Minh's head.

Minh yelped in protest. "Andy said they were too low and tourists wouldn't mind paying more."

"Let me see that." Andy's father took the flyer and examined the menu on the back. "So, Andy," he said, "you think it is fair to have one price for local customers and another, higher, price for foreigners?"

"But it's not a high price for them," Andy said. "Nobody even mentioned the prices. They all thought it was good value. Nobody thought they were being ripped off."

"Answer my question, please. Do you think it is fair to charge foreigners a higher price than locals?"

Andy knew what he was getting at. How many times in Hanoi had he grumbled about the different admission prices for museums, for train tickets, even for the water puppets? In shops and in markets, too, there was always one price for Vietnamese locals and a higher price for foreigners. "It's not fair," he'd complained.

What did he think now?

"Well, I don't think it's totally *unfair*," he mumbled. "Foreigners can afford to pay more and the locals can't, so it's sort of fair to charge what each of them can pay."

"In a restaurant?" his father asked. "What would you have said if at Koto we had been given one menu, with one set of prices, and the Vietnamese at the next table had been given the same menu with much lower prices?"

Andy had to admit that he would have been … well, pissed off.

Minh, who had been listening to their conversation with interest, swooped on the expression. "Pissoff!" she repeated. "I hear tourists say this all time. 'Pissoff,' they say to *bui doi*."

"It is not a polite expression," Andy's father said.

A thought occurred to Andy. "But maybe it's fair to charge more because tourists stay at the table longer. Auntie Mo just said so. They sit around and drink and eat and write postcards or read – remember how you read the paper at that ice cream place by the lake, Dad? And they charged a lot, didn't they?"

"But they charge everybody same price," his father pointed out. "Not one price for locals, higher price for foreigners."

"How you know?" Minh asked suddenly. "How you know they not have two menus with different prices and they give you high price one because you Viet Kieu?"

Andy's father had to admit he didn't know. "But in *this* restaurant," he said, "there is one price for everybody. Isn't that right?" He looked around the table for confirmation.

"Maybe our prices are a little low," Grandma said.

"We could put them up a little," said Auntie Mo.

"Especially if we are turning customers away," said Auntie Thuy.

"What about me?" Minh asked. "Andy says you should pay me for working in restaurant. He said I should be paid celery."

"Salary," Andy muttered.

The adults all looked at him.

"Pay you for work?" Grandma looked scandalized. Who had ever heard of such a thing? Auntie Thuy clicked her tongue.

"Anh has a lot to say about how we should run our restaurant," Auntie Mo said. "Maybe Anh should leave Australia, come here to work."

"No," Minh said. "Better I go to Australia and work. Andy and me could get married."

"What!" Andy yelped. "Where did that idea come from?"

"Married?" His father looked amused.

"Not right away," Minh said. "But tell for immigration, then they let me come."

"I thought you wanted to go to Saigon to be with your mother?" Andy said. "That was the whole idea of Noodle Pie, for tourists to come so you'd get tips –"

"Yes, and for me to get celery, like you said. But they will never pay me celery. You see how they are."

"Can I go to Australia too?" Indy asked hopefully.

Auntie Mo cuffed his ear. "Nobody is going to Australia!"

"Yes, I go to Australia," Minh said defiantly. "Andy say I special girl, deserve special treatment."

Everybody looked at Andy. He shifted uncomfortably.

At that moment, Mrs. Nam burst into the restaurant. She charged up to their table, her face alight. "I come to say thank you," she said. "Those tourists who eat here came to my shop afterwards and bought many, many things. I make a good profit, thanks to you. Tomorrow you want to put out tables and stools, please, go ahead. Take all the space you need. We in the street should all work together." She put some bills on the table in front of Andy's father. "I return money to you, Brother-friend, since I did not lose any business. Thank you again." Off she scurried.

"Well!" said Grandma. "Mrs. Nam returning money!"

"And apologizing!" said Auntie Thuy.

Auntie Mo eyed the money. "I bet she charged those tourists big, big price. She should pay us commission."

Andy said hotly, before he'd had time to think, "You took Minh's tip and now you want to take my dad's money too. He already sends you heaps of money. How can you be so greedy?"

There was a moment's stunned silence, and then Andy's father got to his feet. "Please excuse us. I think Anh and I will go for a walk. We have some things to talk about."

Chapter 15

"I thought we were going for a walk," Andy said.

They had walked to the end of the street in silence, and then his father had approached one of the cyclo drivers who congregated around the intersection and negotiated a rate. For an hour, his father specified.

"Easier to talk and ride than talk and walk," he told Andy. He gestured for him to get in.

If he hadn't been so apprehensive about what his father wanted to talk about, Andy would have been pleased. Cyclos were fun, and something of a luxury. It was far cheaper to hop on the back of a *xe om*, a motorbike, if you wanted to get somewhere, and you got there a lot faster too. But obviously they weren't going anywhere.

"Just drive around," his father told the cyclo driver. The

driver was a lean, sprightly man with a wispy grey goatee, sinewy brown legs and feet encased in socks and plastic sandals. He wore a pith helmet, like many of the old men who strolled around Hoan Kiem Lake, and a faded khaki military shirt. Perhaps he was an ex-soldier? Andy thought he might have balked at the prospect of pedaling two passengers around for an hour, but on the contrary, he seemed delighted. As soon as they were seated, he leaped into the bicycle saddle behind them and pushed off.

Negotiating the intersection was a little hair-raising. Being a passenger in a cyclo was like sitting in an armchair and being propelled into the middle of traffic. There was nothing between you and whatever was zooming your way, you just had to hope the driver pedaling behind you had all his wits about him and years of experience under his belt. But it was too early for the frantic after work rush of bikes and scooters, and their driver seemed competent. He pedaled them around the streets in the Old Quarter. Andy knew many of them quite well by now, but the names were new to him. "That's Bamboo Basket Street," his father said, pointing. "Now we're coming to Roasted Fish Street. This is Sugar Street." *Hang* meant "merchandise," so "Hang Da" meant the street where leather merchandise used to be sold hundreds of years ago. Sometimes the merchandise was still sold there.

Hang Gai was still a good place for cottons and silks. Tailors had been making clothes in this street since the thirteenth century, his father said.

This tourist stuff was all very well, but when was Dad going to get around to the telling-off? It was like being summoned to the principal's office for some offense and then being made to sit and wait while he had a chat on the telephone.

They halted temporarily at what must surely be one of the few functioning traffic lights in Hanoi and were immediately accosted by a street seller waving a pair of fake Ray-Ban sunglasses at them, and another offering maps and postcards. The cyclo started up again before any negotiation could get underway, but the brief interaction must have triggered something in his father's mind because he said suddenly, "So, Andy, tell me about Minh."

"Minh? Like what?" Andy asked, taken by surprise. He'd been expecting the first attack to come from another direction.

"Everything. About her asking for salary, asking for money to go to Saigon, coming to Australia, marrying you." His father glanced at him. "Her idea or yours?"

"Hers! You think I want to get married? Or even think about getting married?"

"I hope not, at your age. But why she say these things? Isn't she happy? Better tell me, I think."

So as the cyclo was pedaled through the Old Quarter and around the lake, Andy told his father about his cousin's alternative life as a street kid. How she'd been skipping school for over a year, selling stuff to tourists – "Look, right over there! See them near the post office? That's where I first saw her" – including the colored pens he'd given her. Andy glanced sideways to note the reaction to this piece of blatant commercialism, but his father's face remained neutral. It was to get money for her fare to Saigon, Andy explained, to live with her mother and to work as a cook in a good restaurant or hotel. That was her ambition. "Like those street kids working at Koto," Andy said. "But Minh's not sixteen, so she can't go there to learn."

"But she learns at Phuong Nguyen," his father said. "Learning on the job. I notice she is already a good cook. And she has a home. She has no need of Koto."

"Even apprentices ought to be paid something," Andy said. "And I guess it doesn't feel like a real home when her mum's not there and everybody treats her like a servant."

"You think she is treated badly?"

"Well, I don't think anyone loves her," Andy said.

"Hmm," his father said, and he stared ahead and tapped his fingers on his knee as if he were thinking deeply. And perhaps he was, because they went right past the grand Opera House, Nha Hat Lon, and his father didn't say, as he had on every other occasion they'd passed it, "Know what that means in English? House Sing Big. Hahaha!"

A scooter driven by a young woman in a dark pantsuit and high heels, a long scarf fluttering behind her and a briefcase strapped on the pillion, suddenly shot out from nowhere and darted in front of them. Andy's heart gave a little jump and he gripped the side of the cyclo as their driver took evasive action and yelled a colorful insult. With one elegant wave of her gloved hand, and without looking back, she accelerated and was soon lost in the traffic ahead.

Their driver was full of apologies. "These modern young women," he grumbled. "They think they own the streets. None of them obey the traffic rules."

It was news to Andy that there were any rules. His father nudged him and winked. "Women drivers," he murmured. "Cabbies are the same all over the world."

Andy was relieved to see this small sign of good humor. Perhaps his father had decided to forget about his behavior at the restaurant. But as they approached the old French Quarter, where the roads were wider and the traffic less frenzied, he said, "Okay, now you tell me all about Noodle Pie."

Andy took a deep breath. All he had wanted to do, he explained, was to show Grandma and Auntie Mo how they could increase their profits. Everybody was working very hard, but how could they make money serving two-dollar banquets to locals? They had to adapt to the market and become more tourist-friendly. Minh understood this. She spoke English, and she knew how to handle tourists.

"I noticed," his father said wryly. "And I know now where she learned this skill."

"Well, anyway," Andy went on. When he got to the bit about the flyers and how helpful Indy had been, his father said, "So Indy is real artist in family. You picked wrong cousin to give those pens to."

"I gave them to Minh because I felt sorry for her, not because I thought she could draw."

"Yes, I realize that. You like your cousin very much, I think."

"I didn't at first. I called her Cheeky. She didn't like me either. She called me Noodles."

"Noodles." His father smiled. "From that came Noodle Pie?"

Andy shrugged. "Sort of. It's just a fun name that tourists can remember. Foreigners can't say 'Phuong Nguyen.' You have to have a name they can say and that they'll remember. You have to translate the menu into English so people know what they're eating."

"You gave a lot of thought to this. Smart boy." His father pulled the flyer from his pocket and spread it out on his knee. "Who is this? That Australian actress?"

"Nicole Kidman, yeah."

"You put her face here to make people think she is a customer?"

Andy didn't want to claim all the credit. "It was Minh's idea," he explained. "Remember that Koto brochure with the picture of President Clinton? She thought we ought to have someone famous on the flyer to impress people."

"But Clinton really did visit Koto. This actress never came to our restaurant."

"Yeah, I know. That's why we don't actually *say* that she's a customer."

"You think that is right thing to do?"

"Why not? We didn't lie, just maybe twisted the truth a little bit. You know, like you did."

"Like *I* did?"

"When you let the family think you were rich. When you told them you were a manager. You said that was just twisting the truth a little bit, that it didn't hurt anybody and made everybody happy. We did sort of the same thing. Nobody got hurt and the customers were okay with it."

"Maybe Nicole Kidman not so okay with it."

"Well, if she complains, I'll take her off the flyer," Andy said morosely. "Anyway, I guess we won't be using it any longer. Grandma and Auntie Mo don't seem that keen on getting big spending tourists into the Phuong Nguyen."

"Ah, Auntie Mo – "

"You'd think she'd see the possibilities. She's always going on about money." Andy kicked the footrest.

"What you said to her was rude and unkind. When we go back you must apologize."

Andy knew he would have to do that. The thing was, he didn't feel apologetic, not one little bit. His clever idea, put into practice with the help of Minh and Indy, had *worked*. Tourists had come, they had enjoyed the food, they had appreciated the service, and they had paid up cheerfully. The long-haired backpacker had even promised to email Lonely

Planet! And it had not cost the family a single cent. Just eight tourists a day would mean a huge rise in profit. Surely they could see that? Instead, they had complained about the tourists taking up room, needing chairs and lingering over meals, demanding extras like napkins and iced water, and wanting to use credit cards. Had Auntie Mo chatted to these new customers in English and made them feel welcome? Had she explained the menu to them and fetched them drinks? Had she shown them how to eat Vietnamese style? No, it was Minh who had done all these things, yet Auntie Mo had taken the tips as if she had a perfect right. It was she who had started the fight with Mrs. Nam, and now she was saying that Mrs. Nam ought to pay them commission if Noodle Pie customers bought things from her shop. How greedy was that? Would she pay Mrs. Nam commission if Mrs. Nam's customers wandered next door to eat at Noodle Pie?

Well, it didn't matter now, because there wasn't going to be a Noodle Pie.

And he would have to go back and formally apologize to greedy Auntie Mo.

It wasn't fair.

Chapter 16

His father folded the flyer and put it back in his pocket, and then glanced at his watch. They had been cruising around the streets for almost an hour. He turned and spoke to the cyclo driver and a little while later they pulled up in front of a *bia hoi* street cafe. "We take some refreshment," his father said.

Bia hoi meant draft beer, the very cheapest kind of beer that was brewed and delivered daily from three Hanoi breweries. You could get a big plastic jug of beer for about fifty cents, and most cafes also sold very cheap food. Chain-smoking men filled many of the tables inside, so Andy sat down on one of the little plastic stools at a low table on the sidewalk while his father ordered drinks and a plate of chicken feet, a traditional snack at a *bia hoi*. He gave Andy a bottle of Saxi, a local drink a bit like sarsaparilla that Andy had developed a taste for, and took a beer and a plate of food over to their driver, who was squatting on the sidewalk next to his cyclo, and lighting up a cigarette.

Andy sipped his Saxi and watched them drink and talk together. His father chatted to everyone – waiters, shoeshine boys, cyclo drivers, boatmen, flower vendors, ticket sellers, girls selling fruit on the streets. He asked them about their lives and their views on the world. At first this had embarrassed Andy. He would shuffle his feet and look away, as if he had no relationship to this person who seemed oblivious to the fact that strangers might not welcome such intrusive questioning. But the odd thing was that they all chatted back. They seemed just as eager to talk to him. Gradually Andy came to understand that it was part of everyday Vietnamese conversation to express an interest in quite personal details, and perhaps the people also sensed that his father was genuinely interested.

His father returned and sat down. He clinked his beer against Andy's soft drink. "*Chuc suc khoe!*" Good health!

"Our driver shouldn't be drinking beer, should he?" Andy said.

His father laughed. "A glass of *bia hoi* won't make him drunk. A jug would hardly make him drunk. Beer very weak. That's why it so cheap. Why aren't you eating?"

Andy wrinkled his nose. "Raw chicken feet! No thanks."

"Try first before you say no. Look. Eat, then drink." His father picked up a claw and expertly crunched off the toes – or

161

were they talons? They looked longer than regular chicken claws. He washed them down with a swig of the beer. "Good eating," he said. "I should have ordered double serving."

The thought of putting a raw bird claw into his mouth almost made Andy gag, but his father was looking at him expectantly, and he figured that the syrupy sweetness of the Saxi would probably kill dead any aftertaste. He picked up one of the feet and gnawed at it tentatively. There certainly wasn't much meat on it, and what little he did manage to bite off tasted unpleasantly gamy. He pulled a face. "I think I'll stick to KFC."

His father laughed. "Real Vietnamese men drink *bia hoi* and eat chicken feet."

"But I'm not Vietnamese, I'm Australian."

"Yes, quite right. And now I tell you the story of why you are Australian."

Not again, Andy thought. He didn't want to appear ungrateful, but he had heard the story of the rusty fishing boat and the pirates and the refugee camp several times before. He knew why he had been born an Australian. Did he have to hear it again?

This time, however, his father told him aspects of the story he had never heard before. Andy had never considered, for example, how much such an escape might have cost, and how it was paid. "In gold," his father told him. "Gold cost us fifteen hundred American dollars, and then we needed extra money for bribes. At river, where we boarded little boat that was taking us to big boat off coast, we had to pay bribes to policemen and officials. So almost two thousand dollars for me to leave Hanoi."

Andy had been in Vietnam long enough now to appreciate what a truly astronomical amount that was. If you were earning only a few dollars a week, what hope did you have of ever accumulating such a sum? "Wow!" he exclaimed. "How come Grandma and Grandpa had that much?"

"They didn't. Very few people had such a sum. Many people on boat had sold everything – houses, furniture – to buy their escape. That's why, when they saw rusty old boat and were frightened it would sink, they still went on it. Because they had nothing to go back for. Everything they owned in Vietnam was gone."

"Did Grandma and Grandpa sell everything too?"

"They sold many things and used all their savings. But Andy, money for gold came from all the family: parents, sisters, aunts, uncles, cousins. Everybody contributed, everybody made sacrifices. You say Auntie Mo is greedy and thinks only of money. Well, as eldest child in family, and probably smartest one too, why wasn't she given opportunity to escape to freedom and a good life? Auntie Mo and Uncle Hop were about to be married. They could have gone together. I am sure she wanted to. Instead, they gave up their future for me. I was lottery winner. But of course it was not really a lottery. Only one person could go, and I was son of family. That was another reason. Vietnam had just declared war on Cambodia. Teenage boys were conscripted into military service and sent off to fight Khmer Rouge. Yes, even boys of fifteen, like me. So you understand why I am grateful and why I owe them so much."

Andy didn't know what to say. He felt deeply ashamed. He had called Auntie Mo greedy. He had resented the money spent on and given to family members, the same people whose contributions had allowed his father to escape to a new life. "Why didn't you tell me this before?" he asked.

"You were young. Difficult for you to understand."

"If I'd known," Andy said, "I would have understood. I wouldn't have called Auntie Mo greedy, or tried to stop you giving people money. I would have given Indy my T-shirt right away when he asked for it. I would have given him *all* my T-shirts."

His father patted his hand. "That's why I didn't tell you. Children shouldn't feel guilty about things that happened before they were born."

A thought struck Andy. "Do you feel guilty, Dad?"

"Yes, often. Gratitude and obligation are big burdens to carry, you know. I think that is part of reason I lied to family about my life in Australia."

"You didn't lie, Dad," Andy said. "You just twisted the truth a bit."

"No, I lied. And now you are doing it. You are following my bad example." He gave a rueful half-smile. "We should call this sort of thing a Nicole Kidman lie and promise not to do it any more, what do you think?"

"A bit tough on Nicole."

"Yes, you are right. She is innocent party. I know, we call it a noodle pie lie."

Andy grinned. "Yeah. And it can be a verb too, as well as an adjective. Like, if you were telling me something and I knew you were exaggerating or telling a fib, I'd say, 'Don't noodle pie, Dad.'" He laughed.

"Smart boy. And when you tell me you want Converse sneakers because everyone in class has them, I'll say, 'I think you are noodle pie-ing, Andy!'" His father laughed heartily and reached for the chicken feet.

A vendor wandered in off the street. He was thin and shabbily dressed, and dangling from a cord around his neck was a plastic tray filled with various bits and pieces. He made a beeline for them, addressing Andy's father as *dong chi*, comrade, and courteously offering his goods. As usual, his father engaged the man in conversation while Andy peered at the odd assortment of things on the tray: plastic shoehorns, a rolled bandage, shoelaces, razor blades, knives, cigarettes, and aspirins which could be purchased individually. His father bought a couple of Band-Aids and told the man to keep the change. "Please do me a favor and have these, Uncle," he added, passing over the bowl of chicken feet. "As usual, I ordered too much."

That wasn't true, Andy thought, but he knew why his father had put it that way rather than just offering the old man something to eat. The man could now accept without losing face. So was that a noodle pie lie?

When the vendor had departed, his father said, "He reminded me of Mr. Tran. You remember Mr. Tran? He has that little shop in Adelaide next to market. He comes from very good family in Haiphong. Servants, bathrooms, nice furniture. And he is educated. In Haiphong he would live like an emperor, but in Australia he has that little shop, working every day and night so he can educate his children and send money home." He nodded towards their driver, who was taking the opportunity to snooze in the front seat of his vehicle. "He owns that cyclo. It cost him two hundred dollars and it took ten years for him to buy. He and his son take turns, so it is in use eighteen hours a day." He looked at Andy. "Know why I am telling you all this?"

Andy nodded. "Sort of."

"Vietnamese people are hard workers. They have to be, to survive. We have had so many wars. After American war – we called it American war, you know, not Vietnam war – this country was a desperate place. Jobs were hard to get, factories closed, essential services near collapse, gas and food rationed. We cut down trees in street for cooking fires. People never forget such bad times, Andy. It changes them. They not mean or greedy, they just a little bit fearful and very careful with money because bad times may come again."

Andy nodded again. He did understand.

"Very different in Hanoi now since I left," his father went

on. "Sure, there are street kids and vendors like that man, but also more opportunities for good jobs, more choices. It has changed most for women, I think. You remember that scooter girl who cut us off? You would never see a girl like that twenty years ago in Hanoi. Now you see business girls everywhere, nice clothes, riding scooters, makeup, high heels. Most cafes and tourist shops are managed by women, have you noticed?"

What Andy had noticed, and it was evident around him now, was that the streets were always full of men sitting on or tinkering with motorbikes, congregating in groups to smoke, drink, chat, or read newspapers. His father was right. Vietnamese women seemed to be the powerhouses of the economy. Was it the same in the Nguyen family? What did Uncle Hop do, for example, when he left early each morning on his motorbike?

"Uncle Hop works as clerk in government department, a good job, and he gets sixty dollars a month. He supports himself, Auntie Mo and Indy, and helps his older sister who looks after their father in village outside Hanoi."

"Oh," said Andy.

His father smiled suddenly. "Hey, don't look so sad. Things are looking up for the Nguyen family. Look at next generation! One smart marketing man, one talented artist, and one brilliant chef!"

Andy tried to smile. "I'm not sad. I guess I'm missing Mum and Mai."

"You feeling homesick, Andy?"

"A bit. Are you, Dad?" He stopped. "I guess you can't really be homesick when you're already home, but you know what I mean."

His father shook his head. "Hanoi is not home for me any more. I have lived in Australia more than twice as long as I have lived in Vietnam, and all my adult life. I am not sure I could live here again. I feel different. I think I must look different too. My aura has changed."

"Your aura?"

His father waved his hand over his head in a vague way. "Whatever it is that signals your inner being, who you are. Until I open my mouth, people here sometimes take me for Japanese."

"Me too!" exclaimed Andy. "Why is that?"

"I have been thinking about this. It must be little changes in way we speak, dress, walk, hold ourselves, how our hair is cut, little things like that. We are Asian but we don't seem quite Vietnamese any more."

"I'm not sure I ever felt Vietnamese," Andy said. "At home I was always surprised when people asked me where I came from."

"And now?"

Andy considered. "I don't know," he said honestly. Despite the claims of kinship and the fact that he was living with his extended family in his father's homeland, he still felt like a foreigner in a foreign country. It occurred to him that this must be why he was feeling a bit homesick and missing his mother and Mai and Dizzy and Hendo – even Mrs. Gowdie!

He could hear Dizzy's voice. "Mate, if you're missing old Gowdie, you're not homesick, you're just sick!"

His father finished his beer. "Time we went back, Andy. Are you ready?"

Chapter 17

Andy made a formal apology to Auntie Mo, in front of everyone. His father said it had to be like that, because he had insulted her in front of everyone. It was not an easy thing to do, but it was made a little easier for him by the fact that he felt genuinely sorry.

To her credit, Auntie Mo received it graciously, even cheerfully. This was made easier for her by the fact that in the meantime she had done a careful accounting of the lunchtime takings and had been startled by the amount. And not just the amount. A significant proportion of the takings had come from the truly amazing quantity of liquid refreshment the table of backpackers had consumed. *Tay balo* might look like penniless layabouts, but they had a prodigious thirst for beer. Tomorrow she would get in some of those foreign labels and instruct Minh to stop offering the cheaper local brands. And really, when she had had time to think about it, the *tay balo* had been no trouble. They were friendly and uncomplaining; they were used to squat toilets; they didn't carry on about people smoking – oh yes, she had seen the looks of disapproval from that *ba tay*, that Mrs. Western Tourist with her big bottom. Still, you didn't get a big bottom or an enormous stomach from eating like a bird, and Mrs. Western Tourist and her husband had munched their way through several of the more expensive dishes. Even the barbarians, the girls with the bare legs and pointing feet, had been generous in paying the bill, and then, apparently, they had gone straight into Mrs. Nam's and spent even more American dollars.

All in all, it had been a satisfying afternoon. Why should she hold a grudge about something her nephew had said in ignorance and in the heat of the moment, especially since he had allowed her to regain face? And especially since it had been his clever idea that had brought tourists to the restaurant? Yes, she would forgive him.

"I, too, have something to say to everybody," said Andy's father, getting to his feet.

Andy, who had sat down feeling very relieved it was all over, now looked at his father with some concern. His voice had been tense, nervous even. What announcement was he planning? Couldn't he just let the matter drop?

He glanced around the room, the same room they had been ushered into when they'd first arrived. The benches had been pushed back against the walls, and biscuits and tea had been set out on a central table. Minh, who was seated on the floor munching a biscuit, caught his eye and pulled one of her cheeky faces. Her expression seemed to say, "What you said about Auntie Mo was true, we both know that, but you made a nice apology."

"Have some tea and biscuits," Grandma urged her son. "Look, they come from Malaysia. There is no need to say any more about Anh."

"This is about me." Andy's father cleared his throat.

Everybody looked at him expectantly.

Uh-oh, Andy thought.

"It is time I told you the truth. The whole truth," his father began. "And the truth is that I am not a successful and wealthy businessman. I am not a businessman at all. Back home in Adelaide I work for the city, that's true, but I am not head of a department. I am a gardener."

His family looked at him, and then at each other. A gardener? Andy's father repeated the word in English, so that Andy would be sure to understand what he was saying.

"Does this mean the same in Australia as in Vietnam?" Grandma asked. She mimed someone digging with a shovel.

"Growing plants," said Auntie Mo. "Digging in the dirt."

Andy's father nodded. "Lots of digging in the dirt. That's the part I like best."

They looked baffled.

"I'm sorry I let you think otherwise. I knew you wanted

to be proud of me, to boast of my success to the neighbors, and I too wanted you to be proud of me. I couldn't tell you how hard it was when I first arrived in Australia, alone, and not speaking English. And I didn't want to worry you. I knew things were hard for you back here, too. So …" He shrugged. "I painted for you a rosy picture."

"You are not rich?" Grandma asked.

"I am not rich. Lien and I both have to work very hard to pay our bills. I had to borrow money to come here."

"But the gold watch, the diamond ring?" Auntie Thuy said.

"They are not mine. I borrowed them."

There was silence in the room.

"I am sorry I am not the big success I pretended to be. Please forgive me."

Again, the silence. It was clear nobody knew how to interpret this new information, or how to react. Andy looked at his father. He stood with his arms by his side, his face apprehensive and embarrassed.

Andy jumped to his feet and went to stand by his father. His words flowed out in a jumble of English and Vietnamese. "You want to know the truth about my dad? The truth is that he *is* successful. He's probably one of the luckiest and most successful men in the whole country because he's doing a job he loves and that he's brilliant at. He started as a laborer, and now he's a senior gardener in the Botanic Gardens. In a few years' time he might be in charge of all the parks and gardens in the whole of Adelaide –"

His father gave a little cough. "Andy, I think you might be noodle pie-ing."

"Dad, I said you *might* be in charge. That's not a noodle pie lie."

The family murmured among themselves. Noodle Pie again … What was this Noodle Pie business? Was Tuoc starting a restaurant in a garden?

Andy forged on. "And he's also successful because Mum and Dad and Mai and me are a happy family. We haven't got a lot of money but we've got a house and a car and we're all together. My sister and I go to a nice school and my teacher Mrs. Gowdie says if I apply myself and work hard I can go to the university. Mai, too, I guess, except right now she wants to be a bus driver. So even though he's not a rich businessman, I just want to say that you did the right thing when you all helped him to escape to Australia, and my sister and me are really grateful, and you can be proud of him, because he's the best dad in the world."

Had they understood all that? His father had, because his eyes were wet and he was hugging Andy, something he very rarely did.

Minh had, because she was pulling a friendly, cheeky face at him.

Indy had, because he was giving Andy a thumbs up.

Auntie Mo must have understood, because she was rapidly translating for Uncle Hop and Grandma and Grandpa, and they were listening and nodding.

His grandfather spoke. In English. "Anh, you smart boy." It was a phrase he must have heard his son use, and his English did not go much further. The old man beckoned to Minh, who jumped to her feet and went over to him. He spoke to her quietly in Vietnamese.

Minh turned to her uncle and cousin and translated. "Grandpa say his father also planted things and digged in the earth. He say there is no shame in that. Only shame is not to live honest life."

Looking straight at his son, the old man spoke again, and again Minh translated his words, her small face screwed up in concentration.

"Grandpa say money and diamonds not important. More important to be happy in work and have strong family. He say you are your father's diamond, Andy."

There were murmurs and nods of agreement, and Andy felt his father squeeze his hand.

Minh grinned impishly. "Perhaps I call you Diamond now, not Noodles?"

Andy, pink with embarrassment but with a warm feeling inside him, said, "Nah, I'm sort of used to Noodles."

"Ah, noodles," said Auntie Mo. "Noodle Pie. You know, I think it would be a good idea for us to make tourists more welcome. We could certainly put out some chairs and tables, practice our English …"

"*My* English," Minh muttered under her breath.

"The flyer that my son did," Auntie Mo went on, "was

number one quality." Indy beamed. "We should distribute more around the neighborhood and places tourists go."

"I can do that," Indy volunteered. *Anything to get out of school.*

Andy's father cleared his throat – he seemed to be having trouble with his voice – and said, "One more thing. It's about Hien and Minh." Everybody looked at him expectantly, especially the two cousins. "My father is right, and I thank him for reminding me," he said, with a slight bow in the old man's direction. "Children are our diamonds, our investments for the future, and I would like to do something to help these two here. If you stay at school, nephew, and pass your exams, I will help your parents to get you proper training in art or graphics, if that's what you want. Would you like that?"

Indy nodded vigorously, and Auntie Mo and Uncle Hop looked pleased, too.

"Minh, I understand you want to be a chef and work in a top hotel restaurant?"

Minh darted a quick look at Auntie Mo. This was an ambition she had kept secret for a long time. What would happen if she said that, next to seeing her mother again, it was what she wanted most in the world? Auntie Mo was looking very agreeable right now, but that was because of two things: first, Indy had been promised a good education, and second, she had belatedly realized there was money to be made from catering to Western tourists. And for that, she would need Minh's help.

"Minh, is this what you want to do?" Uncle Tuoc was

asking her again. "There is an excellent restaurant college in Adelaide. When you are older, you could stay with us and train there. Would you like that?"

Andy was looking at her, a little frown on his face. "Tell them," he murmured.

Suddenly their grandmother spoke. "Minh should do this," she announced. "Cooking is a family skill, I learned from my mother and Minh has learned from me. But Hanoi is changing, and new skills are needed. Granddaughter, don't pass up this chance my son offers you."

To his surprise, Andy understood every word.

Minh took a deep breath. Her eyes shining, she said, "Yes, I like to do that very much. Thank you, Uncle."

"But first you must complete school," Uncle Tuoc said. "Do you understand? Is that agreed?" He looked at her so meaningfully that Minh realized he must know about her activities outside the post office.

"Okay, deal," she said.

"In the meantime," her uncle went on, "I think it would be a good idea if you came to Saigon with Andy and me for a few days. It's time you saw your mother again, and I too would like to see my younger sister."

"You take me to Saigon?" Minh's face was suffused with joy.

"We're going to Saigon?" Andy asked, surprised.

"Why not?" His father smiled at him. "You have met your Hanoi family, now you should meet your Saigon family."

"Well! You are a lucky girl," Auntie Mo said.

"Yes, lucky girl," Minh agreed happily. She and Andy grinned at each other.

"It's been a big day," Andy's father said. "I think we all deserve a night out. Can we close the restaurant?"

"We have to close the restaurant," Auntie Mo said. "There is no food left! Those big-eating tourists cleaned out the kitchen!"

They all laughed, especially Grandma. "Cleaned out the kitchen!" she kept repeating.

"Indy can write a sign to say we are closed," Andy suggested.

Auntie Mo waved her hand. "We can just pull down the door."

Andy shook his head. "No, that's not customer friendly. We should put up a sign that explains why we're closed, and that encourages customers to come back. Like …" He thought for a moment. "Closed due to successful afternoon trading. Please come again tomorrow."

Everybody nodded approvingly. "Anh smart boy," his grandfather said.

"Where we go tonight?" asked Minh excitedly. "Maybe a number one restaurant?"

"I'd like to go dancing," said Grandma, quite unexpectedly.

"Dancing!" Her son looked at her in surprise. "It's been a long time since you went dancing, Ma."

The old lady nodded. "There used to be a nice place near West Lake."

"About a hundred years ago," Minh whispered to Andy. He grinned.

"All right, we'll try to find it."

"And after that," Andy suggested, "could we go to Fanny's for ice cream?"

His father shrugged in cheerful resignation. "Dinner, dancing, ice cream – why not? I am a rich man."

Noodle Pie
Recipes

Method and ingredients

There's a lot of **slicing and cutting** in Vietnamese cooking, so you need **sharp knives** and a cutting board. (Depending on your cooking experience, you might need some help with all the slicing and cutting and, later, with the frying and grilling.) Vegetables are sliced on the diagonal, and each piece should be small enough to be picked up with chopsticks and eaten whole. If your slices are all the same size, they'll cook at the same rate and stay crunchy. Meat is cut into strips across the grain.

You should be able to buy the **ingredients** easily at any Vietnamese shop or market. Buy fresh food on the day you're going to cook, and keep a supply of things like rice, fish sauce (*nuoc mam*), dry noodles and vermicelli, bean sauce (*nuoc tuong hot*) and spices in your food cupboard. Fresh herbs like mint, coriander and basil are used a lot. They are easy to grow in pots, and that way you'll always have a ready supply.

Vietnamese cooks use a **wok** (*chao*) over a charcoal fire for almost every kind of cooking: stir-frying, dry and deep frying, steaming, making pancakes, etc. A wok works better on a gas burner than on an electric one, so if you don't have a gas stove, use an ordinary frying pan. In **stir-frying**, the small pieces of food cook as you stir them quickly around a very hot wok. If you stop stirring, the food will stick. If the wok is not hot enough, the food will become soggy.

Vietnamese eat with **chopsticks** and also cook with them, instead of using forks, tongs, spoons and spatulas. (But it doesn't really matter. Use whatever you feel comfortable with.)

Dishes are served all together and eaten with **boiled rice**, usually white long grain rice.

How to cook rice (if you don't have an electric rice cooker):

Place the rice in a large saucepan with a heavy bottom and a close fitting lid. (Two cups of uncooked rice will serve 4 – 6 people.) Add cold water until it is an inch or so above the level of the rice. Stir in some salt and bring to a boil over high heat.

Boil for a couple of minutes, gently stirring to prevent the rice at the bottom from sticking. Reduce to a simmer, put the lid on, and continue cooking until all the water has been absorbed (15 – 20 minutes). Don't lift the lid!

The rice can sit like this for about 30 minutes, or even longer, before serving.

Easy Recipes

Fried bean sprouts with pork and prawns
(Gia xao)

2 cups bean sprouts

3 ½ ounces raw shrimp meat

3 ½ ounces pork fillet, sliced thinly

1 onion, cut into thick slices

1 clove garlic, crushed

2 tbsp oil

2 tbsp fish sauce

Chopped spring onion

Handful cilantro leaves

Heat the oil in a wok or frying pan, and add the onion and garlic. Stir-fry for a minute or so until the onion is soft and translucent, then add the pork and the shrimp. Stir-fry until cooked, about 5 minutes. Add the fish sauce and bean sprouts and stir-fry quickly, but don't let the sprouts get too soft.

Sprinkle the spring onion and cilantro on top before serving.

Cold spring rolls *(Goi cuon)*

10 rounds of rice paper, about 5 – 6 inches diameter

10 small leaves of butter (soft-leaved) lettuce

3 ½ ounces rice vermicelli, fresh or dry

10 cooked shrimp

10 slices of roast pork, thinly sliced

Fresh mint leaves

Slice the shrimp lengthwise. (So each shrimp gives you 2 pieces.) If using dry vermicelli, cover it with hot water until it softens, and then drain. Briefly dip each rice paper into warm water, then lay them on a kitchen towel, ready to stuff and roll.

Place 1 lettuce leaf, 2 pieces of shrimp, 2 or 3 mint leaves, 1 heaped tablespoon of vermicelli and a slice of pork in a neat pile at one end of the rice paper, then roll it up tightly, turning the ends in to make a neat package. As you finish each roll, cover it with a damp cloth so the rice paper doesn't dry out.

Serve with dipping sauce (*nuoc cham*). The recipe for this sauce is on the next page.

Dipping sauce *(Nuoc cham)*

4 tbsp fish sauce

2 tbsp rice vinegar

2 tbsp sugar

Fresh lime (or lemon) juice

1 tbsp finely chopped red chili

1 tbsp finely chopped garlic

Combine fish sauce, vinegar and sugar with ¾ cup water in a saucepan and bring to a boil. Reduce heat, add lime juice, and bring to a boil again for 2 minutes. Take off heat and let cool. Stir in the garlic and chili.

This makes enough dipping sauce for 10 cold rolls. The sauce will keep in the fridge for 2 – 3 weeks.

Vietnamese chicken salad *(Ga xe phay)*

In a bowl, assemble the salad:

Half a boiled or roast chicken, shredded

1 cup Chinese cabbage, shredded

1 or 2 handfuls of bean sprouts

2 long red chilies, sliced (be careful!)

4 spring onions, sliced

Baby salad leaves or arugula

Shake all these ingredients together for the dressing:

2 cloves garlic, chopped

2 tbsp fish sauce

2 tbsp brown sugar

3 tbsp lime or lemon juice

2 tbsp oil

Toss the salad with the dressing. **Garnish** with crushed peanuts and fresh mint and cilantro leaves.

Fried beef with watercress salad *(Bo luc lac)*

Watercress (or any salad mix)

1 pound lean fillet steak

Combine these ingredients for the marinade:

5 cloves garlic, crushed

2 tbsp oil

1 ½ tsp sugar

Salt, pepper

Cut the steak into 1-inch cubes. Cover the steak with the marinade, and put it in the fridge for an hour or longer to marinate. Meanwhile, prepare the onion mix.

Mix together:

1 large onion, cut into thin slices

2 tbsp vinegar

2 tbsp oil

1 tsp sugar

Salt, pepper

Heat some oil in a wok or frying pan over high heat. Add the marinated meat and stir-fry for 2 – 3 minutes, until just cooked.

Arrange the salad on a plate. Put the cooked meat on the salad, and pour the onion mix on top.

Garnish with chopped spring onions or chives.

Street Kids in Vietnam

Nobody knows just how many children are trying to survive on the streets in Vietnam, but one of the last estimates for Hanoi put the figure at 23,000. There are almost certainly many more than this. Street children are everywhere, begging and selling on street corners, rummaging through garbage, curled up asleep on the sidewalk at night. The appalling conditions in which they live and work make the heart ache.

One person who has helped many of them to new lives is Australian Jimmy Pham. Saigon-born, he established the training restaurant Koto – Know One Teach One – in Hanoi in 2000. From a small cafe, it has grown to an eighty-seat restaurant run by Vietnamese staff and forty trainees – former street kids – who, after training, go on to good jobs in the hospitality industry.

The registered charity Street Voices, established in 1998 by Jimmy Pham and other caring Australians, raises funds and accepts donations for the Koto kids.

You can learn more at the website **www.streetvoices.com.au**